Harry Sue

sue stauffacher

ALFRED A. KNOPF
new york

THIS IS A BORZOI BOOK PUBLISHED BY ALFRED A. KNOPF
Copyright © 2005 by Sue Stauffacher
All rights reserved under International and Pan-American Copyright Conventions.
Published in the United States by Alfred A. Knopf, an imprint of Random House
Children's Books, a division of Random House, Inc., New York, and simultaneously
in Canada by Random House of Canada Limited, Toronto.

KNOPF, BORZOI BOOKS, and the colophon are registered trademarks of
Random House, Inc.

www.randomhouse.com/kids

Library of Congress Cataloging-in-Publication Data
Stauffacher, Sue.
Harry Sue / Sue Stauffacher. — 1st ed.
p.   cm.
SUMMARY: Although tough-talking Harry Sue would like to start a life of crime in order to
be "sent up" and find her incarcerated mother, she must first protect the children at her
neglectful grandmother's home day-care center and help her paralyzed friend.
ISBN 0-375-83274-2 (trade) — ISBN 0-375-93274-7 (lib. bdg.)
[1. Mothers and daughters—Fiction. 2. Separation (Psychology)—Fiction.
3. Prisoners' families—Fiction. 4. Friendship—Fiction. 5. Paralysis—Fiction.
6. People with disabilities—Fiction.] I. Title.
PZ7.S8055Har 2005
[Fic]—dc22   2004016945

Printed in the United States of America
June 2005
10 9 8 7 6 5 4 3 2

For my dear friend, Suzie MacKeigan, whose
generous spirit has embraced many a girl like
Harry Sue

All you fish, listen up. I'm talking to you. While you're sitting there, cooling your heels in the tank, you might as well know the story of Harry Sue. Everything moves slower here. It's like walking underwater. Time, my friend, is something you have too much of, and you'll learn that a story well told—even if it's full of joint jive you can't fully comprehend—is worth more than all the personals you collected on the outs. Especially if it lifts you out of your skin.

You got a lot to learn if you intend to survive the joint, and finding the right teacher is no easy matter. Everyone wants to play you on the inside. Maybe you think the cast-off child of two convicted felons is not a good bet. Well, you'll soon find that on the inside, up is down and left is right.

Or maybe you're a buster, the kind who raises

his hand and says, "I'm no fish, Harry Sue. What are you on about?"

My answer to that is plain and simple: "Yes, you are." I don't mean *fish*, fish, fool. I mean fish. New to the system. And if you still don't follow me, go on and look it up on the next page so you don't fall behind.

Now I know I can count on at least one waterhead to say, "There must be some mistake, Harry Sue. I have no intention of getting on the wrong side of the law, let alone being sent to the joint."

Whoever said it was a choice?

It's time you learned something for real. Not all prisons have four concrete walls and a steel bunk. I say prison is a lot like home. It all depends on where your heart is.

Language gets out of prison every day, Fish. You may already know some slammer slang from your life on the outs. But just in case you get tangled, here it is:

Harry Sue's Joint Jive Glossary

all day: going to prison for life

backstory: the story of how you got to prison

bug: go crazy

bumpin' your gums: talking too much

burn the spot: ruin the moment

buster: a jerk

Category J or **J-Cat:** a person who is or acts crazy

catnap: a short prison sentence

cell warrior: a con who talks a good game from his cell but backs down outside it

change: some part of a year

cheese eater: a tattletale. What eats cheese? A rat, of course.

click: to gang up on someone. "Click up" means to join a gang.

con: a male convict, prisoner

conette: a female convict

Conglish: a combination of joint jive and English

cooling your heels: waiting

couple up for count: an order to prisoners to pair up to be counted

crew: the gang you hang with

crumb snatcher: little kid, toddler, child

deuce: a two-year prison sentence

dime: a ten-year prison sentence

ding wing: the mental ward

direct order: a command from an officer

doing time: living out your sentence in prison

down letter: letter saying you don't get parole

dragon's tongue: the overcooked roast beef they serve in the prison cafeteria

drop a dime: tell on another con

dry up and blow: disappear

ear hustle: eavesdrop

eight ball: an eight-year prison sentence

eyeball: when a con stares down a guard. It's a bad idea.

eye hustle: see something you're not supposed to

fish: a new prisoner

flat-talkin' fool: a con or conette who talks nonsense

foo foo: anything that makes you smell sweet, like after-shave or perfume

funky: smelly

gas house: prison bathrooms

get shanked: get wounded by a shank

give it up: share information

gladiator fight: a fight to entertain the other cons and show you're tough

green light: when a prisoner is marked for death by other prisoners

hack: a prison guard

hard time: a long, hard sentence, usually for cons who don't play by the rules

hog: a prisoner who won't back down from a fight

hole: solitary confinement in prison

home release: when you get out of prison for a little while

homes or **homey:** short for "homeboy" or friend

inside: in prison

it's on: a challenge, a call to fight

joint: prison

joint jive: prison language

joint mentality: so used to being bossed around, you don't try to fight

KO: knockout

lay it down: start a fight

lockdown: when prisoners have to stay in their cells during a crisis

low pro: keep a low profile, keep it secret, between two road dogs

mad-dog: mess with by insulting

MCC: Metropolitan Correction Center, a big-city prison. If you have a choice, don't go here.

monkey: another name for a guard

nick: a nickname for "nickname" . . . get it?

nut up: go crazy

on the low: keep it to yourself, a secret

outs: life on the outside

PC up: when a con or conette asks to be put in protective custody because he or she's afraid

personals: your stuff

play you: fool you

put grass under your feet: walk away from a conversation

R & D: receiving and departure—coming in and going out of prison

rap sheet: a list of your crimes

rat: a tattletale

retired: a life sentence without a chance of getting sprung

road dogs: the friends you know you can count on

roadkill: cigarette butts cons pick up by the side of the road when they're part of a cleanup crew

sent up: sent to prison (in some parts of the country, it's "sent down")

shake the spot: leave

shank: a homemade knife or other homemade weapon

shower hawk: a con who gets you in the shower

signifying: showing your gang colors

snitch: a tattletale

special-handling unit (SHU): pronounced "shoe." Solitary confinement.

sprung: get out of jail; be released

super-max: joints with the most security—"super-maximum"

tailor-made joe: a brand-name cigarette

tangled: confused

tank: a holding pen where new prisoners are held

tat-sleeved: arms covered with tattoos

tight crew: same as road dogs. Your closest friends.

T-Jones: a prisoner's parents

toss out: search a prison cell

waterhead: a prisoner who says stupid things

yard: a place outside for prisoners to get exercise

yellow brick road: the yellow line that marks the edge of the yard. Cross it and you might look like Swiss cheese.

yoked: prisoners with lots of muscles; built

yokin' up: lifting weights

Part 1
Revenge

The Wicked Witch was so angry when she saw her black bees in little heaps like fine coal that she stamped her foot and tore her hair and gnashed her teeth. And then she called a dozen of her slaves, who were the Winkies, and gave them sharp spears, telling them to go to the strangers and destroy them.

—*The Wizard of Oz*

Chapter *1*

Harriet Susan Clotkin is not the sort of name you'd imagine for the first lady president of the United States. That's just fine by me, as I never had designs on running for political office but planned instead on following in the family tradition: a career of incarceration. As soon as I was old enough, I was headed for the joint. First I had to have the required fourteen to sixteen years of rotten childhood. So far, I had only served eleven years and change.

Time was running out on my becoming a juvenile delinquent. The really impressive cons started their rap sheets by nine or ten. Unfortunately, I had a heart condition that needed fixing before I could begin a serious crime spree.

Yes, Fish, my heart was as lumpy and soft as a rotten tomato. I couldn't stand to see things hurt, especially anything weak and defenseless. Watching Jolly Roger and his road dogs pull the legs off a spider made me grind my teeth down worse than if I slept with a mouth full of sandpaper. When those boys clicked the little kids on the bus, I had to sit on my hands just to keep from breaking theirs.

In the joint, where I was headed, I'd need a heart filled with cement and covered in riveted steel. I was working on it. But so far, I wasn't making much progress.

Now, there's a thing or two you need to know if you want to do time with Harry Sue. First off, you got to keep it real. Most everybody I know, they just see what they want to see. Aside from my road dogs, the people I have to deal with—including my teacher, Ms. Lanier, and that bunch over at Granny's Lap—they just see my mask.

It's like my favorite book, *The Wizard of Oz*, which just so happens to be the last one my mom read to me before she was sent up. Most people, they have only ever seen the movie. But me, I read the book. Twenty-seven times. If you didn't read the book, then you think it's all about singing and rainbows and skipping down the Yellow Brick Road.

You don't know anything about the real story. In the real story, those horrible winged monkeys help

Dorothy. They do! And the Tin Man murders forty wolves, and when Dorothy gets to Oz, the Munchkins think she's signifying because her dress has white in it and that's the color of witches. There's monsters in that book whose names you can't even pronounce right. And they're not in any dictionary, either, because I checked.

There's so much they don't tell you in the movie. And people don't think to ask afterward. They just take what they see as the real story.

Me, I'm a little like Dorothy myself, searching for my own Aunt Em. I don't care where I have to live when I find her. It's been six long years since I set eyes on my mom. Some days, it feels like she's as far away as Oz is from Kansas and like I'll never see her again. In the real story, they don't have any of that hokey-pokey crap where Aunt Em calls out, "Dorothy! Dorothy! We're looking for you!" from the magic crystal ball.

The real story is more like my life. You have to wonder what Aunt Em is up to while Dorothy's trying to get out of Oz. Is she going through the motions, milking the cows and shucking the corn? Or is she wrung out with grief, sitting paralyzed on the back step, her eyes fixed on the flat line of horizon?

Chapter 2

Life at Trench Vista Elementary School was something like doing time. There was "the yard," what the principal, Mr. Hernandez, liked to call the courtyard. It sat next to a playground that pushed up against the wet edges of Marshfield's water treatment plant.

On days with a northeasterly wind, we were marched to the playground to play kickball, freeze tag, and other games designed to use up our energy. But on days with a southeasterly wind, when the smell from the treatment plant filled our nostrils and made more than one kid remember what became of lunch, he'd hustle us into the courtyard for jump rope and four square and tetherball.

That's when I felt the closed-in, clamped-down

feeling of prison. I'd pace the edges of the yard, ducking in and out of the ragged lilac bushes and honeysuckle vines that were planted as a pathetic defense against the smell of Marshfield's liquid garbage. Our sixth-grade year was only thirty-eight days into a nine-month stay, but I knew things were heating up considerably. There are days when I can feel the trouble in my bones.

Violet Eleanor Chump was what we considered the lowest form of life in the joint: a snitch, a rat, a cheese eater. Old Violet would drop a dime as easy as batting her eyelashes. Since Mr. Hernandez was particular about keeping the students in alphabetical order—to line up for recess, to line up for chow, to line up for the buses—I spent more time around Violet than I'd've liked. I had to sit next to her, too, and there wasn't much chance of that changing unless an eleven-year-old with a name between Chump and Clotkin had the misfortune to enroll at Trench Vista.

Fish, don't make me say this twice. If you want to hang with Harry Sue, you got to learn to do your own time. It was hard to imagine anyone choosing to go to school at Trench Vista. Yet here we were by accident of birth—or maybe just plain accident, as in my personal case. But if you have to be here, stop messing around in other people's business and attend to your own.

Violet's problems were mostly due to her notion

that she was special. She thought someone should care about how she felt. She thought her needs mattered. *What kind of family did she grow up in?* I wondered.

I was filing back in after recess, observing the rule of "closed lips, hands on hips," when Ms. Lanier put a bony hand on my shoulder and pulled me into the coatroom.

"I'm afraid those," she said, pointing to my soggy shoes and holding out a plastic Family Fare grocery bag, "will need to stay in here.

"It's possible we'll need to have a talk about personal hygiene, Harry Sue, and the importance of bathing on a regular basis. You are getting older now and your body is undergoing changes."

Ms. Lanier put one finger inside the tight collar of her blouse and pulled it away from her damp neck. I had a sudden image of Granny loosening jellied cranberry from the can with a long-handled butter knife. At Granny's Lap, we ate canned jellied cranberries as a fruit serving from December to March because it was cheaper than dirt and made most of the crumb snatchers want to heave. Whether you ate it or not, it still counted as one fruit serving for Granny to put on her federal forms.

Ms. Lanier's neck quivered in just the same way the cranberry did as she stood there contemplating my body undergoing its changes.

I kept my eyes to the floor. Somewhere in my chest my heart started to throb as I knelt to untie my shoes. They were cheap and worn, the kind you pick up in the bin next to the flip-flops at Value Village.

The pounding inside me was so loud it threatened to give me away. *She would bathe regularly,* it throbbed, *if there wasn't always a baby in the bathtub. The shoes stink,* it complained in its trembly way, *because we had to haul Spooner from the pond again this morning.*

I caught my breath, checking for the mask, letting it handle the damage control. My jaw set, I looked up at Ms. Lanier, imagining my gaze passing through an invisible magnifying glass, like sun does, heating it to the burning point.

It worked. Suddenly, we were just two conettes on the yard who didn't have permission to take it outside. Ms. Lanier looked away, but I kept the gaze on her, not bothering to glance down at the laces disintegrating between my fingers.

It was the best look in my catalog and I used it a lot. I called it "mad and dumb." You didn't want to appear too intelligent. What you wanted was a look that said: *This dog bites.*

"Violet has a very delicate constitution," Ms. Lanier said. "On bad days like these, what with her asthma and her allergies, she just can't take the added assault on her senses."

She removed the finger from the collar that was choking her and shook open the bag. I held the stare as I dropped the shoes into it.

"Socks, too," she squeaked.

Did she really expect me to spend the afternoon barefoot?

Before I could think what to say, she dipped down and picked up a pair of wool socks, man-sized, from the bench we used to remove our boots. Then she grabbed her can of Fruit Fresh Peachy Keen aerosol spray and proceeded to douse my new socks with the sickening-sweet scent of factory-made fruit smells.

I focused my stare. Little dewdrops of sweat formed in the tiny hairs above Ms. Lanier's mouth. Without breaking my gaze, I peeled off my soggy socks and dropped them into the grocery bag.

My temples were throbbing and the bone that ran between my neck and my shoulder, the one that never got straight since the fall, was pressing against a nerve. What was it about Ms. Lanier that always made things hurt worse? The pain made me think of a line from Mom's favorite fairy tale, "Jack and the Beanstalk," where the giant tears apart the kitchen looking for the kid who's been lifting his golden eggs.

I'll grind your bones to make my bread.

The entire class was twisting in their seats, straining to get a view of my entrance. I tried to look dignified with a pair of man's socks dragging at my ankles. A couple of busters in the back row covered their mouths and pointed.

"If anybody laughs, it's on," I hissed.

But then I told myself not to get distracted. What was most important was to find Violet. I needed to communicate with my eyes my look that said:

Somewhere, somehow, when you least expect it, I will exact my punishment.

Chapter 3

Before we go any further, we have to go back. Way back. Seven years back, to the day of my accident. You can't fully appreciate the saga of Harry Sue unless you know the backstory. Every conette has a backstory. It's hard enough returning to the night that changed my life forever, but if it was up to my road dog, Homer, we'd go back even further.

You see, Homer would argue that my father, Garnett Clotkin, didn't just show up to our apartment that night swearing and spitting like a rabid dog for no reason at all. Not everybody expresses their anger with violence. Garnett had to be trained to it.

"Maybe your granny tied his shoes too tight,"

he'd offer, or, "Maybe it was her habit of dunking his head in toilet water when he sassed her."

I say, any way you slice it, it's still bread.

On the night that changed our lives forever, the man I called father was nursing a wounded pride by drinking up as much Motor City Ale as he could locate. He wanted my mother to take him back. She'd already been down to the police station to get a restraining order to keep him away from us.

To me, anyway, that meant, "I don't think so."

But to my father it was just a piece of paper. He was too much of a man, too lit on Motor City Ale, to use that restraining order for more than what kept his chewing gum from sticking to the bottom of Granny's wicker wastebasket.

To make a long story short, Mom threatened to call the cops when he barged in, so he dangled me out the window to get her to pay attention.

"I'm warning you, Mary Bell. Put the phone down."

People say I couldn't possibly have a clear memory of that moment. I was only five years old and barely conscious. He'd pulled me out of that little-kid sleep, the real satisfying kind that comes from not knowing the score.

But I do remember. I remember her crying, "Don't hurt my baby! And how the air felt, so wet it was like fingers pressing on my face. And how it smelled—both sweet and sour—like the garbage under our sink in summer.

I heard and felt all those things before I was yanked back inside.

After that, it's a blur, but I can tell it fairly from the way the neighbors whispered and from the trial. Mom connected to the Marshfield Police Station and started talking gibberish. My father, being a man of his word, picked me back up, pressed my knees to my shoulders, and shoved me out the window, using the chest pass that kept him in school until the ninth grade as first-string guard for the Trench Vista varsity basketball team.

That is the kind of detail Homer loves because it shows how everything, every action, affects what comes after. Homer likes to say if my dad had chosen baseball over basketball, he'd have to call some other dog his best friend, for I would be long gone from this world.

Because he was a basketball player, my father squished me into a ball and launched me out the window when his instincts took over. His anger was like rocket fuel, enough to catapult me into the branches of an elm tree. See, an elm tree is shaped like a vase, so instead of dropping seven stories to the brick patio, I began a long, slow-motion game of pinball, rolling toward the center of the tree. This is another detail Homer loves, because if it had been an oak tree, well, we've already touched on that possibility.

I do remember the sensation of wet branches grabbing me, of leaves slapping my face. I rolled all the way to the center of the tree before it let go just ten feet from the ground and dropped me onto a pile of wet leaves and soggy mulch.

In the time it took me to ride that leafy elevator to the ground floor, my father's head cleared enough to determine he'd just committed a capital offense. Who knows? Maybe he even felt bad about it, at least bad enough to lay me on the backseat of his truck and rush me to the emergency room, where I was diagnosed with a severe case of bruising, a dislocated shoulder, and two broken ribs.

Mom rushed out, too, but he'd copped the elevator and she couldn't match him for speed down seven floors. In all the confusion, she forgot to put away the toy chemistry lab she'd set up on the table to make crystal methamphetamine, or crank as it's called on the street, an illegal drug she mostly used herself to stay awake while working the swing shift at the auto glass factory.

Homer has a field day here. If Mom didn't have to work swing shift, if she hadn't recently started selling to her co-workers, if it wasn't so darn easy to make the stuff with ingredients you could buy from the mail-order drugstore. If Garnett could have found it in his heart to pay a little child support. If any of these things were the case . . .

The fact is, the police officers weren't looking for drugs, but for a madman throwing children out the window. They might have thought it was sugar left over from baking a cake if she hadn't also left the chemistry set right there, and the order form, written out on the sheet intended for my kinder-garten submarine sandwich sale.

Left it, just sitting on the table for all to see.

So while my father was explaining what happened to the ER nurse—swearing up and down that it was the first time and he'd never do it again!—my mom was dragged, kicking and screaming, down to the police station and booked for production of an illegal substance with intent to distribute.

You know what, Fish? Sometimes, in my dreams, I am back in that elm tree. It is playing catch with me, tossing me back and forth in its soggy branches. And always, I am being tossed downward. That's why I feel so terrified. Not because I'm falling, but because of *where* I'm falling. I'm falling straight down, down, down, into Granny's Lap.

Granny is the one who caught me, not really caught me, but the one who got me straight from the hospital. She seemed like the perfect choice. She'd been operating Granny's Lap, her in-home day care, for over ten years.

On a nice day, I will tell you there is something wrong with Granny, something that happened maybe in her childhood that twisted her heart into a knotted noose. On a bad day, I'll say she's evil and greedy and ranks right up there with cockroaches and the tetanus shot on the list of why *did* God make such things?

When Granny realized that there'd be no assistance money since she was a blood relative, and that I'd take up a slot that could no longer be filled by a paying day-care kid, she tried to give me back. Using the famous Clotkin chest pass, Granny shoved my face into the tweedy plaid jumper worn by the caseworker assigned to decide my fate.

I could see the woman was plain horrified by what she had to do, but Granny was my closest blood relative and she'd proven she was capable of taking care of kids, now hadn't she?

"I want my mommy," I cried as we shuffled down the wide waxy hall of the courthouse. Granny yanked me into the ladies' room and cocked her purse. She was going to whack me with it. Granny loves clouting kids. I'd go so far as to say it was one of her hobbies, she gets so much pleasure out of it. You can whack a kid real good on the back of the head and it won't bruise like a slap on the face.

But she didn't hit me. And that was the only time in memory she looked to be heading in that direction.

Why Granny didn't hit me was, for quite some time, beyond my understanding.

Her friend Serafina, who does tarot reading on bingo night down at the senior citizen center, was convinced by my aura that I was in the constant presence of spiritual beings. I heard her yakking about that once at Granny's kitchen table.

But I will tell you right now, Granny didn't buy that.

No, I believed that since Granny wished I didn't exist, she just did everything in her power to make it so. In all the time I lived with her, she only admitted I was in the same room maybe half a dozen times. That was when she was too angry to keep her story straight. Only twice did she speak to me directly. And that was when things were too far gone to keep from bumpin' her gums.

It was the best excuse I could give for why she never patted my head or put her arm around me or gave me a peck on the cheek. On the plus side, it also meant no clouts, no kicks, no pinches, and no head dunks, either. The closest I got to Granny's lap was touching the words printed on the sign in her front yard.

I have to say, on the whole, if all the world's got to offer you for a little hug or some comfort is Granny, I prefer to go it alone.

Sure, I made it out of the bathroom that day

without a mark, which is more than I can say for most of the crumb snatchers who tangle with Granny. But some things hurt more than a meeting with the bottom of Granny's purse.

"Oh, baby, I am so sorry." That's what Mom said as she held me for the last time before her sentencing. "Your mom is so sorry." She held me tight enough to take my breath away, but I didn't care. Finally, she took hold of my shoulders and looked me in the eye.

"I gave you two things, Harry Sue. They're going to have to hold you till I get back, honey."

"What things?" I asked, tears just falling down my face.

She looked over at the lady judge, who, far as I could tell, was sucking her lips between her teeth to keep from bawling right along with us.

The judge nodded and called a five-minute recess.

Mom knelt down and looked me straight in the eye. "I read to you, didn't I? And you're smart as a whip. You didn't start slow like me. You're gonna be somebody, Harry Sue."

She shook my shoulders on that last part, like she wanted to shake the idea all the way to the bottom of me.

"And I gave you your name. You aren't the kind to invite trouble, so I had to do it for you. You need practice to stand up for yourself properly. No girl named Harry Sue gets pushed around. She's the kind that goes down fighting."

Mom was looking over my shoulder now, past the lawyers and the social workers. Was she looking at Granny?

"*Nobody's* gonna tell a Harry Sue that she's nothing."

"You hear me, Harry Sue?" Mom insisted. "You got those wishes from me folded up inside you. They'll have to hold you till I get back," she said again. Like I didn't hear her the first time.

That judge came over and laid a hand on my shoulder.

Granny sat in the back of the courtroom filing her nails.

"I hate her, Mom," I said, squinting, trying to see clear.

"I hate her, too, sweetie. But that'll have to be our secret."

And she didn't tell me to mind Granny, either, because we both knew that would turn me into something worse than if I just minded myself.

Chapter *4*

The other thing you need to know is how we landed here in Marshfield. Because the house was big and cheap and Granny had to put distance between herself and the bad publicity. Having a family scandal wasn't the best advertisement for a day-care business. We only moved two counties over, but in Marshfield, Granny could put her own spin on things.

The most important person in Marshfield was a boy named Christopher Dinkins. You think I haven't mentioned Christopher before. You'd be wrong there. Because Christopher Dinkins is also Homer Price.

It's the very same thing in *The Wizard of Oz*. If you just saw the movie, then you believe there's only one good witch. But there's two. And the first, most important one didn't look like a poufed-up Barbie doll. She was old and gray and wrinkled. Nothing like a fairy princess. I guess that's why she got cut from the script.

He was Christopher when I met him, standing at the bottom of Granny's long gravel driveway, watching the big kids get off the bus.

I don't remember exactly, but he says I was asking each kid in turn: "You gonna be my friend or what?"

He was two years older than me, which made a big difference at five and seven.

"Go on," said the boy he was hanging with. "Go play with your dolls or something."

"I don't have any dolls," I answered.

"Say, you aren't that kid . . ." Another one stopped and poked at me with a stick.

People said that a lot to me back then.

Christopher grabbed the stick and broke it off.

"Come on, then. Tell us. What did it feel like? Have you blinked it out or what? Did it feel like flying?"

I studied my grimy little nails, making them wait.

"Not exactly flying. Nope. Something different."

Christopher said it was the look on my face that brought him back around later, after he'd ditched his friends. He knew I was holding back. Even back then he looked at everything just like a scientist. And falling seven stories was about the most interesting experiment he could think of.

He let me tag along while he was thinking up things. Not to any of the places he hung out with his friends. We never went by the creek that led into the swamp, the baseball diamond next to the Presbyterian Church, or Sweetland's Candy Store. No, there was never a crowd in Christopher's thinking places. He needed quiet. So we sat in the hollowed-out trunks of silver maples or behind tangled curtains of black raspberries whose thorns discouraged most people from wandering in our direction.

He was puzzling out how things worked. Might be he was dissecting one of the crank pencil sharpeners we had in school or maybe a broken toaster he'd scored out of somebody's garbage can.

He liked to talk it through, see? Scratching in the dirt with a stick, he'd come up with what he called "add-ons." An "add-on" made an item better than it had been before. He wanted to be the first to get a patent on the machine that would butter your bread after it had been toasted. And he figured out how to make a pencil sharpener that emptied itself into the garbage so you didn't get all those dirty shavings on your fingers.

Christopher always said I made the best kind of company when he was inventing because I asked smart questions. But I could also stay out of the way if need be.

Even back then I felt like I had time on my hands, waiting as I was for Mary Bell to come back and get me. It would never do to call Granny's Lap home, so I had to get comfortable with other places. And I did. Over the years, I roamed the open spaces of Marshfield with Christopher and, when the weather was bad, I hung around with his mom, Mrs. Dinkins, holding the other end of the sheets as she folded them or being her "go-for-it" girl when her arms were elbow-deep in dough. Where Granny was mad just because I took up space, Ariel and Gerald Dinkins seemed to have room for one more.

Or at least that's how it seemed. She trimmed my hair and he taught me how to ride using Homer's old bike. She baked me a birthday cake and he sang "Happy Birthday" just like Donald Duck.

But it's a dangerous thing to call someone else's family your own, Fish. Some part of me refused to let them take the place of Mary Bell. And after what happened to Christopher, it was a good thing I held back.

Where I loved to be more than anywhere else was Mrs. Mead's garden. Christopher took me there not long after I landed in Marshfield. We didn't go by the road or through our yard to hers—

as she lived right next door to Granny—but through the little patch of woods that separated Mrs. Mead's house from the Palmers' house on the other side.

"Check this out, Harry Sue," he said, pulling me down on my knees. I looked at the ground and saw a plant with leaves like green butterfly wings. Next to the plant on the ground were what seemed to be shriveled marbles, all caught up in a green string.

"It's a twin flower," he said, touching the little marbles carefully. "After it blooms and makes a seed, the stem wraps around the seed and curls it back down toward the earth. Most plants just let go of their seeds, but this here's a plant that doesn't like to take chances." He smiled at me through the curls that always hung down over his eyes.

I pressed the seeds to show I was listening, but then I stood up. Something made me want to go forward. That day, I felt no patience for studying such things, so I left Christopher leaning over that plant in wonder, and kept on my way. Farther down the path, I rounded the corner of an old garage and was surprised to come upon Mrs. Mead herself, kneeling over the ground and poking little holes in the earth with her finger.

"My land, you surprised me," she said, pulling together the collar of the bathrobe she wore on cold days. I remember that bathrobe. It was heavy and white and made out of some shiny material that made it sparkle in the sun. And it seemed like the least practical thing to wear for digging in the dirt.

"I'm planting the lettuce and the spinach today, Harry Sue," she said, like she'd known me all my life. "But I do have trouble getting up. Give me a hand, dear."

I grabbed her free hand and turned to offer her my good shoulder to lean on.

"It's a pity I'm not as strong as your granny," she said, grunting a little on the way up. "Now let's hold it just a minute. Steady."

We stayed still like that for a long time so Mrs. Mead could stand on her own without tipping.

"What a good girl you are! I might have been down there all day." She took my face in both her hands and kissed me right on the forehead. It left a big wet mark. I wanted to wipe it off, but for some reason I didn't.

"Now, now, it's not as bad as all that," said Mrs. Mead, studying my face. "And it will have to do for when I'm not around."

None of what she said made any sense, which must be why I always remembered it. But I liked that I could come to her garden if I wanted to. Granny didn't allow much socializing with the neighbors, but in July, when the pole beans and the sunflowers made a forest out of a flat place, I would sneak over to Mrs. Mead's while the crumb snatchers napped and lie down right in the middle of it. It felt safe to dream of Mary Bell in Mrs. Mead's garden and of how things would be when she came back. And for some reason, it was always easier to conjure up thoughts of my mom there than anywhere else in Marshfield.

I'm only telling you this, Fish, because it's important to make sense of things. You need to know the backstory. About my accident and how I landed in Marshfield. And how it was with Homer and me. Before. Everybody has a backstory, Fish. Garnett, Mary Bell, Homer, me. Remember that when you're eyeballing a new con. The real story starts somewhere in the past.

Chapter 5

First thing I do when I get home from school is take Moonie Pie out of the bathtub. It is written in the crumb snatcher code of conduct that nobody messes with me until Moonie Pie is out of the bathtub. Granny sets him there for his nap because she doesn't have enough proper beds. To Granny, it's a bathtub when the drainplug is in and a crib when the drainplug is on the counter. She doesn't have enough proper beds because she regularly takes four or more kids than she's licensed for.

Granny has two voracious habits that she feeds by cramming kids into every corner of this house. The first one, straight up, is bingo. Granny loves to gamble. The second is China Country, her curio cabinet of limited-edition ceramic figures that she orders off the Home Shopping Network. Granny calls them her pretties, a whole planet's worth of stuff locked up behind glass in the dining room. There's a little peasant boy and girl bending toward each other to get a smooch, a squirrel with a tail made out of real fur just about to bite down on a ceramic nut, a milkmaid and her cow, and a princess with a starry-eyed look just waiting for her prince to come.

That is the same look I got from Moonie Pie, who was so grateful to be sprung, he gave me a sleepy grin that lit up the moldy corners of the room. His little feet were ice-cold. I grabbed the booties he always managed to pull off and wasn't halfway down the stairs before the rest of the bunch attacked my knees.

"Tell us a story, Harry Sue. Please! Tell us something."

"All right, all right. I'll tell you something. Let. Go. Now."

On a regular day, there'd be nine crumb snatchers hanging all over me. Including the babies, Syl and Moonie Pie, there was, in order of their age: Hammer Head, Wolf Man, Princella, Beanie, Carly Mae, Tiny Tim, and Zipper.

Granny was nowhere to be seen at the moment, and her live-in help, her nieces Synchronicity and Serendipity, were out back stealing a smoke. Of course, that left the kids to their own devices. Yes, nine children under the age of six alone in a house, completely unattended. If you can't stomach that thought, you'd better close this book right now because it's going to get a lot worse.

Mostly they were a sorry bunch. Even if they worked together, they couldn't bring me down. Maybe Hammer Head if he caught me off guard. But Granny attracted mild kids, punks who were easy to boss. Soon as lunch was over, all they could think to do was hang out at the windows waiting on me to get home and issue some direct orders.

"Couple up for count," I said, handing the baby to Princella and shrugging out of my backpack. I made sure I could see 'em all, nobody off poking their fingers into light sockets.

"Okay, okay. Wanna hear 'The Three Little Pork Rinds'?"

"Tell me about a princess," Beanie said, tugging on my shirttail and gazing up at me with her big brown eyes. Beanie was all fins and gills, Fish— that's right, a brand-new conette—and she hadn't memorized all the rules.

I shook my head.

"A pretty one."

"No princesses. Just conettes."

"What's a conette?" Beanie wanted to know.

"Wolf Man?" I nodded in the direction of a four-year-old with a sorry mop of hair.

"Thath a female convict," he said, pulling his

thumb partway out of his mouth. "Boyth are conth and girlth are conetteth."

" 'Red the Hood'! 'Red the Hood'!"

" 'Beauty and the Hack'!"

"No! 'Padlocks and the Three Bears.' "

"I want all the traps shut *now*," I said. I needed a minute to think.

It was Beau, Homer's home health aide from the county, who taught us all about life on the inside. Beau was fluent in Conglish, had smoked his share of roadkill, and knew the convict's code by heart. He was schooled, Fish. And not from watching movies, either. Beau came to Marshfield directly following a stint at an MCC down near Chicago where he did an eight ball for two counts of grand larceny.

Beau taught us the importance of telling a good story. It wasn't enough to like stories. It wasn't enough to read them to yourself. You had to learn to master them. A good storyteller had power on the inside because she could wound without a weapon.

She could strike an invisible blow with her mind.

That was the reason I told the little crumb snatchers a story every day. You see, Granny and I were locked in a war for control of the joint. My aim was to shut her down for good. Put up a Closed sign on the front door. Soon as I knew the crumb snatchers were sprung from Granny's Lap and she wouldn't be able to terrorize any more little children, I could begin the crime spree and the poor decision making that would land me in the joint.

As I have already mentioned, it was past time for me to begin the running away, the life on the streets, and the petty criminal activity that is the hallmark of your average conette. I needed more contact with the system, maybe an abusive older boyfriend who sold drugs and a couple of years of eating out of Dumpsters if I was ever going to make it to a correctional facility.

Since I had no idea where my mom was, I might have to check into two or three joints before I found her. That's why I felt a pressing need to get started.

I pulled Moonie Pie onto my lap, not because I'm soft, but because he was funky. His diaper should have been changed about the time I was switching sugar for salt in the teachers' lounge at lunch recess. Bathing isn't required in the joint, so I had to get used to funky. Other than that, touching is strictly forbidden.

The heart is too soft, remember? Cuddling babies is no kind of way to tough up.

Moonie Pie was awful quiet, and even though he looked at me, he didn't seem to really register. It was half-past three and he could hardly lift his head, which probably meant that the hacks were giving him cold medicine again.

Everybody gets a nick in the joint and hacks are no exception. I called Synchronicity and Serendipity hacks because that's another name for prison guards. But beyond that, they each got a personal nick. Your personal nick comes from the name on your birth certificate, your old neighborhood, the way you look, or your reputation from your days on the outs.

I nicked those girls "Sink" and "Dip" because on a normal day they didn't share a sensible thought between them. I didn't have to look far. The girls I have to call cousins—on my father's side—had the nicks right inside their names: "Sink-ronicity" and "Seren-Dip-ity."

There's a program on TV about child development, and that psychologist says that teenagers are like one-hundred-pound toddlers. Just trying to satisfy their needs. That seemed to describe Sink and Dip to a tee. I often wondered how bad their own mom must have been to make them choose to live with Granny after they dropped out of school. Sometimes, I suspected they were just used to being pushed around. They were just crumb snatchers, plus a hundred pounds.

Like everything else in life, you have your good hacks and your bad hacks. "Granny's little helpers," as she called them in front of the parents, were mostly lazy hacks. If they put a spoonful of cold medicine in the applesauce, they scored three hours of uninterrupted nap time to dish about friends, watch soaps, choose their personal fashion colors, and smoke tailor-made joes out by the swing set.

I laid Moonie Pie down in front of me to let him sleep it off.

I'd deal with the hacks later.

"All right then, sit down. The first thing you should know about Red is she wasn't little."

The crumb snatchers got quiet in a hurry. Carly Mae sighed and started sucking her thumb.

"She was six-feet four, two hundred pounds, and she could press five hundred on a weak day. And she was a *hood*. As in hoodlum, lawbreaker, conette, not fit for decent society. When her mother gave her those cakes and that bottle of wine to take to her old granny, Red called up Prince Charming and they polished the bottle off not fifty yards from the cottage.

"Next up, they ate the cakes and went crying back to mommy with a story 'bout how they'd been chased by a giant rabbit until the bottle was broke and the cake was just a bunch of crumbs."

"I not afraid of a rabbit," Wolf Man declared.

"This was no ordinary rabbit. This was Peter Rabbit, and he'd done four years and change in super-max on account of he couldn't stop breaking and entering into Farmer McGregor's garden. Now he sharpens his teeth on a garden hoe."

Wolf Man looked unsure, like maybe he wanted to take back what he just said.

"He's your garden-variety criminal," I told him, driving home my point. "Where do you think they came up with that phrase? Hang around that element and you'll be sleeping on a steel bed with no mattress.

"Okay, then, where was I?"

"Telling a story about Prince Charming," Beanie said, rubbing her eyes.

"Right. They were full of hot air, of course, but Red's mother, whose birthday was about . . ." I looked into the sky and tapped my finger on my chin.

"Yesterday!" the crumb snatchers yelled in unison.

". . . yesterday, gave Red another bottle and more cake, which was only enough to make her tipsy and sprinkle crumbs on the bottom of her stomach. So when she finished that, she stumbled down the road to see what she could score off Granny."

"What about the printh?" Wolf Man asked. "Wath he one of her road dogth?"

"No, he wasn't her road dog. You think Red would pick a crybaby like Prince Charming to be her road dog? No. Definitely not. Prince Charming was not in her crew. She just kept him around for giggles."

Carly Mae took her thumb out of her mouth. "We're a crew," she said, beaming up at me.

She was right, of course. These little hair balls were my crew, which was a problem, really. Between Homer, who couldn't lift a finger . . . literally, and this sorry bunch, I had almost no protection at all. My back was feeling the breeze.

"So she ditched the prince," Hammer Head prompted. He had no patience for getting off track.

"We're in the forest, right? And Red is stepping on every toad she sees."

"That's mean," Beanie said.

"The criminal element," I replied, sighing, "have a tendency to be mean."

"I'm telling ya to shut up," Hammer Head leveled at Beanie. He had a way of silencing a crowd. He was five and bigger than the other kids, but there was something about the way he walked into a room and where he sat—always a few feet from the crew—that suggested he was one of those dogs who preferred life on his own to the pack. His nick came from an unfortunate incident involving a cousin and a Tetra-Tom Transformer. Don't come between Hammer Head and what he wants or he'll use the top of his head like a battering ram.

"Red was so busy uprooting wildflowers and pulling the wings off butterflies that it looked like she didn't see the big old wolf sneaking up on her.

To his eyes, she was just a sweet little something out picking flowers for the afternoon."

"But you said she was big," Carly Mae blurted out, in spite of herself.

"Yeah, you can't change the thtory," Wolf Man complained. Even Moonie Pie was waking up now, following the sound of my voice. I waved my hand over his face and he reached up to grab it. Carly Mae had inched closer and closer until she draped herself, like a wet blanket, on my bad shoulder. I let her stay there because it hurt something terrible when she pressed down like that, and I had to learn to keep going through the pain if I had any hope of connecting up with Mom again.

"The wolf saw Red's big old arms and he thought, 'Chicken wings!' as he rushed right in for the kill. No pleasant chitchat like in the other story. That's for little kids.

"But Red, she'd done some time in super-max—stemming from that assault conviction on Cinderella—so she'd known the wolf was there all the time. In the joint, as you know, you grow eyes in the back of your head. In about two seconds she flattened that wolf with the brass knuckles she always wore on her right hand and as he lay there in the dirt, all mangy and twitching, fleas buzzin' like crazy, she had a thought. . . ."

"Yum, yum," said the crumb snatchers, and rubbed their little bellies.

"Sure enough," I said, pleased they'd remembered. "She ate him. He was a little dry going down, but he was filling.

"'Shame to get halfway to Granny's,' Red said to herself, waddling down the path, 'and not know if she's finished up that latest batch of elderberry wine.'

"So Red made her way over to Granny's. When she got there, Granny wasn't in bed like they always tell you. No, she was lying on the couch with a beer in one hand and a racing form in the other, trying to figure out which horse to bet on in the ninth.

"'Granny, what a big old bum you have,' Red said in greeting."

Now, at this point in the story, I used a high, cracked voice, not unlike that of our own Granny during R & D—receiving and departure—when she's trying to act the part of a dear old lady who cares.

"'The better to lie around gambling and ignore my charges,' Granny replied.

"'Granny, why don't you get off your bum and get me one of those drinks you have stored. . . .'"

Here was where I always slowed down so the crumb snatchers could fully absorb what I wanted them most to remember and to repeat later to their parents.

"'. . . some of that caustic stuff you keep

stored—in full view—of the crumb . . . children, right there under the sink. The Drano,'" I said. "'Yeah, that's right. The Drano from under the sink. I'll take a glass of that, seeing as I've got a little tickle in my throat.'

"Truth was, that wolf's tail wouldn't stay in Red's stomach and get digested. It kept poking back up into her mouth.

"'Aw, Red, get it your own sour self, would ya? Can't you see I'm busy?'"

What I didn't mention was that I always checked that the child-safety locks I'd swiped from the Rylee's Ace Hardware Store were latched on the cabinets under the sink. So there wasn't much chance of any accidental poisonings while I was at school.

But my plan was to discredit her. The poison under the sink planted seeds of doubt. I was working up a lush garden of doubt regarding Granny's abilities.

I looked out at the kids blankly, having lost my place with my wanderings.

"Red wath going for the Drano," Wolf Man prompted. "She wath gonna get rid of that plug in her throat."

I patted Wolf Man's head. He must have passed on the applesauce at lunch because he was all there. Wolf Man remembered every line of my stories. If he lived on the other side of town, he might be enrolled in one of those Young Five programs they advertise on the cable access channel, with music and art and circle time. Maybe some nice speech therapist would help him with his lisp.

"'Get it yourself, Red!'" I cried out, pushing away the thought of Wolf Man with a decent haircut and a backpack and taking on Granny's lunatic voice again.

"'Climb on the counter and get your own glass. . . .'"

"Oh, children," came the sickening voice of the real Granny, wafting into the room like a bad cooking odor.

"It's that blessed time of the day when you depart from me. Goodness, look at the time. Synnnnchronicity! Serrrrrendipity!" she howled. "Get in here!"

It was time for the Greatest Show on Earth and nobody'd changed into their costumes yet. A collective shiver went through the little crumb snatchers at my feet. I took in their stunned, wide-eyed stares as Granny swaggered into the room smelling like cheap cigars. She had a can of lemon-scented furniture polish in one hand and a cashmere cardigan in the other.

On the face of it, she looked like your garden-variety old lady: white hair pulled back, wrinkly arms, red cheeks from a bunch of busted-up veins. When no parents were in view, she kept her wardrobe simple: black sweats and a sweatshirt that read Riverside Athletic Club.

See, for an old lady, my granny was built. She lifted weights and walked on her treadmill four times a week, not to mention all the upper-body work she got dangling crumb snatchers over the toilet.

But when the parents came around, Granny yanked on some hose and threw on a dress that looked like it came right out of the 1950s. Yes, she looked to all the world to be a proper, pearl-chokered little old lady. But at that moment, as she stood in front of the crumb snatchers in her sleeve-less dress, her eyes and her biceps bulging, my granny looked like the dragon lady, who, at any moment, might belch fire.

With a practiced "grab and pull," she lifted Carly Mae to her feet. I tensed, ready to spring, as Carly Mae burst into tears. This would most defi-nitely have earned her a clout if Sink and Dip hadn't entered stage right.

"You stink!" Granny howled, aiming the spray at their hair.

Pssst! Pssst! went the can. Granny dropped Carly Mae and swooped down. The crumb snatch-ers ducked in unison.

Grabbing a balled-up apron, she swatted at Sink and Dip.

"How many times I told ya, watch the clock!"

Dip shrank away as Granny landed a fistful of apron on her head. Then Granny grabbed a thick book of nursery rhymes that also doubled as a blunt instrument when she was mad. Sink scurried after Dip.

Struggling into her cardigan, Granny belted out directions:

"Put that cinnamon crap in the microwave! Where's the art project?"

Her eyes cruised past me. "Something stinks in here! I want it gone!"

As if I were what was wrong with this picture.

I just smiled and stayed where I was.

"Where's the art project?" Granny repeated, spraying more polish into the air. She gave Sink and Dip a withering look as we heard the first beater turn onto Granny's gravel driveway. Smoothing her skirt, she yanked back the curtains.

"Here it is." Sink came flying back into the room with the stiff pile of painted sunflowers that Granny'd scored off the kindergarten art teacher at the end of last school year. But Granny barely glanced at them. She threw the sheaf of sunflowers in the direction of the kids, who ducked again before hurrying to pick one up and step back in line.

"But my nameth not Bob," Wolf Man had the poor sense to protest. Granny's eyes narrowed in fury. She looked like she was going to knock the girls' heads together.

"You didn't cut off the names?" she asked in a low, controlled voice. Which was actually worse than when she was screaming. She took the sunflower out of Wolf Man's trembling hands and tore it in half, looking into his eyes with her look that said, *Make a comment like that again and I'll tear you like this picture.*

But there would be no more verbal harassment from Granny today. Carly Mae's mother, Wanda, opened the door without knocking.

"Where's my girl?" she said. Wanda drove a delivery truck and suffered from heaving boxes around all day long. The way she walked, you could see her mind was not so much on her child as on her own aching back.

"Oh, dear," Granny said, sighing heavily and fixing her hair back into place for Wanda's benefit.

"No more duck, duck, goose today, children." She smiled sweetly.

No more duck, duck, Granny today, children.

"Will you look at the time? We finished our art project just in time for the paint to dry."

This was by far the part of the day I hated most, though I had to admit Granny had the routine down pat. That slightly harried, loving-grandmother accent, full of sugar and spice. Most of the parents fell right into her trap, wanting so bad to believe they could get down-home love for their kids at Granny's quantity-over-quality prices.

But Carly Mae's mother wasn't one of them.

"Cut the bull, Granny," she said as she walked into the room. "Let's see your hands, kids."

The crumb snatchers dutifully held out their hands.

"Just like I thought. Not a drop of paint. Not even under the fingernails." Carly Mae's mom squeezed Hammer Head's hands before she dropped them. She was one of the few people he would let touch him. Old Hammer Head had a soft spot for Wanda.

She took the painting in Carly Mae's hand and shoved it back at Granny.

"Keep it," she said. Then she took hold of the fist Carly Mae didn't have shoved in her mouth and scooped up her daughter's precious teddy bear, Oswald.

"And next time, try a little harder," she called before slamming the door.

Sink and Dip cringed again, but Granny wasn't troubled. Wanda might take Carly Mae out of Granny's Lap as soon as she moved up a pay grade, but there were more where Carly Mae came from. Always more.

Granny ordered Dip to microwave the apple cider spices. Sink combed the kids' hair.

"Now, what did we do today?" Granny quizzed them.

"Uhhh, finger playth?" asked Wolf Man.

44

"Dress up?" Beanie said, catching on quick. Granny rewarded her with a tight-lipped smile.

"Baked bread," Hammer Head said, smiling up at Granny.

She looked at him with suspicion.

"With a nail file in it."

Way to go, Hammer Head, I cheered him silently. If anyone could lead the prison break, it would be Hammer Head. When the day came, he was my right-hand dog.

There's a saying about how you grow old quickly in the joint. Though he was only five, Hammer Head was double that age on account of the things he'd seen and done. Not that he let on about it. His face was what showed the score.

All in all, they made good cons, I thought proudly. They lined up carefully for R & D. They knew how to grease a deal.

And every single one of them had their fingers crossed behind their backs.

They understood about the mask.

"Don't forget story time," I said, speaking up for the first time. "And little Red and Granny and all the wonderful things Granny has stored under the sink."

We locked eyes, Granny and me. For the second time that day, I used my look that said,

Somewhere, somehow, when you least expect it, I will exact my punishment.

But Granny was a hog, not at all like Ms. Lanier or Violet. Granny didn't look away. Her upper lip stayed dry as toast.

One by one, I watched them go, until all the crumb snatchers were accounted for. Wolf Man's mom showed up at last.

"Knock, knock," she said timidly. He dropped rank and threw himself into her arms.

"Now, I don't want anyone to hold supper on account of me," I said to Sink and Dip, breezing past them on my way to the door. The first shift was safe for another day, and the third shift didn't come on until eleven. For the next six hours, I was on home release.

Chapter 6

At this point in the story, you may have questions. You may wonder things, things like, just where is my mom? How come I know so much about the joint when I've never done time? Why don't I report Granny to some kind and caring social worker and just be done with her? Here's your next rule, Fish. Don't get personal.

If a conette wants you to know something, she'll tell you. Otherwise, leave it alone. Don't look at her personals unless she invites you. That's right. Don't pick up a photograph, don't touch a letter, don't ask about her mother or her boyfriend, don't even look her in the eye unless you want to lay it down.

And if you value your life, don't ever, *ever* ask about what happened to her father.

As a fish, you should know that every piece of information you give to another con or conette can be used to hang you. Be straight, but don't offer up any more rope than you have to.

So if you got questions, just hold your tongue in your hand. Squeeze it if you have to. Anyone headed for the joint needs to learn to be patient. Time is the one thing a con has too much of. You'll find that cons will waste time, kill time, just spill it on the ground.

I still had time on the outs, so this was a concept that got me tangled. But Homer knew all about con time, and that's where I always headed when I was sprung from Granny's place. Right to the tree house of Homer Price.

Course, I'd have to get past Homer's mom, and that was no easy prospect. But Homer and me were road dogs from way back, so I made the effort. Homer's real name, as I have mentioned, was Christopher Dinkins, but I gave him his nick after the crack inventor in the book. Homer's nick came from his habit of dreaming up inventions, and, before the accident, building them, too.

But that was all before he got slammed with, not a deuce, not an eight ball, not a dime, but an all day. . . . Yes, it's true, Fish. Homer Price maxed out with a life sentence for the crime of diving off the Grand Haven pier.

I didn't bother with the front door, just went

around back. Through the kitchen window, I could see Mrs. Dinkins standing with a coffee cup in her hand. She was staring in the direction of the tree house. I'd seen Beau's old beater at the curb, so I knew Homer wasn't alone.

Even though he was a home health aide for Ottawa County, Homer said Beau was part of the crew.

"I don't think you can get much closer to a person than when he gives you a sponge bath" was how he settled it.

Whatever. I liked Beau. He taught us how to get along on the inside as well as on the outs. We felt comfortable with Beau—Homer and me—so I thought maybe I could get away with just a wave to Mrs. Dinkins, haul myself up the rope, and spend some time with Beau and Homer, learning how to handle life on the inside.

I made a big circle with my arm as I ran past the window. I guess I knew it wouldn't work, and I was dead on with that guess. The screen door slammed before I could grab the first knot of rope.

You see, after the accident two years ago everybody pretty much figured old Homer was a goner. His lungs kept filling up with fluid and there were other parts that stopped working, too, right along with his arms and legs. When the Shooting Star people came around to grant him a wish, he didn't ask for an expensive trip or anything. What he wanted was a tree house, way up in the most ancient oak in Marshfield, which just so happened to be in Homer's backyard.

He wanted a tree house with a lift and a big picture window cut in the roof so he could concentrate on where he was going and not so much on where he'd been. Homer wanted to spend his last days in the sky.

For real? He mostly wanted to get away from Mrs. Dinkins, who had started to look like one of those statues with parts of her worn away from too much touching. Mrs. Dinkins was always worrying some piece of her own self, rubbing and rubbing like she was trying to erase the body that made the boy who caused so much grief on account of his foolishness.

Getting away from his mother was a full-time occupation, especially after Homer refused to go to the school for the handicapped over in West Olive. After that Mrs. Dinkins was both his mother and his homeschool teacher. The very thought of Homer laid out flat with Ariel Dinkins at his side trying to puzzle through cell biology made Trench Vista Elementary seem almost bearable.

Now she hurried after me, pinching her side like she'd been running and got a cramp.

"Harry Sue," she said, all breathless. "Stop in after, won't you? And visit a minute?"

What she really meant was, *Stop in and tell me: Is it a bad day?*

She wanted to know his mood always. After he came down for the night, would he talk with her about the books they'd been studying the evening before? Would he care about the gossip she brought back from her daily walk?

I had tried to explain to her about letting Homer do his own time.

Poor Mrs. Dinkins was crazy with sadness over what had happened to her boy. Christopher Dinkins had been a great athlete, a classroom mastermind, a streetwise con. Now he was as wobbly as a beat-up con, laid out on a stretcher, watching birds through a hole in the roof.

"These books you been bringing him," she said, rubbing her thumb and her pointer finger back and forth on her jaw. "I don't think they're doin' much good."

"I just get what he asks me to," I said quietly, backing away. I didn't want to get her going.

She kept stepping forward to keep us in talking distance. Just my luck, Beau must have finished wiping and turning and airing out Homer, because right then he started climbing down the rope. We both studied his tall lean frame like it might tell us something important. I don't know what.

Beau nodded to me after he touched down,

breathing as steady as if he'd just walked across a parking lot. I didn't know his nick from the joint as that was something he chose not to share. But if I could give him one, I think it would be Tin Man. After eight years and change, Beau had learned to live without a heart. He wasn't mean. Far from it. He just didn't seem attached to anything, didn't get flustered or upset. He was a master at controlling emotion.

I wanted to be like Beau was, just before he left for Chicago, looking off into the distance and talking to us as if he were talking to himself.

"There's some trouble back home, and I'll be gone at least a few days," he said slowly, running his hands up and down the length of the rope. "My brother called. Gangbangers gone and marked the house where my Mama lives. Homer says he'll be fine till I get back."

Mrs. Dinkins sucked in air and started with the questions.

"Have they assigned a replacement? Who's gonna be able to climb that rope? Homer don't take kindly to people who pry in his business. . . ."

Beau silenced her with a look.

"Said Homer'll be fine till I get back."

Mrs. Dinkins stopped in mid-sentence and began to iron the sides of her dress with her palms.

"You say so, Beau, then I know it's true."

I got another short nod before he walked over to

his car, got in, and drove off, all in that slow dignified way that said he wasn't afraid of nothing,
wasn't in a hurry, wasn't even angry with whoever
marked his mama's house, just needed to take care
of business.

"A man's got to do what a man's got to do,"
Mrs. Dinkins said, looking after him. "For his
mama."

"That's for real," I said under my breath, and
started to haul myself up hand over hand. "See ya,
Mrs. Dinkins."

She was like a ball and chain, I thought as I
climbed, happy to be rid of her.

No, her sadness was even heavier than that. It
was so big it pushed Mr. Dinkins out of their home
and back to his brother in Indiana. It grew like one
of those yeast experiments we performed in school,
consuming all the sugar in its path. Homer was hiding out from it high up in this tree. But he knew and
I knew there was no getting away from Mrs. Dinkins and her pain. Mrs. Dinkins was just the kind of
person the Wizard had in mind when he tried to
talk the Tin Man out of his plan to get a heart. You
see, some folks are so tenderhearted, they have no
business with having a heart.

Shaking Mrs. Dinkins always made me feel
lighter, so light I didn't even use my legs as I hauled
myself up to Homer's tree house. Being *built* was
part of my plan.

While most of his so-called friends couldn't see their way clear to visit Homer, I found being with him the most relaxing part of my day. Homer was my road dog. Unlike the crumb snatchers at Granny's Lap, who were fish and new to the system, Homer was thirteen and he'd been in the joint for two years and change already. He knew what it meant to do time. And he understood why I had to do it, too.

It was Homer who got me started with my notepad, just a small seventy-nine-cent pad of lined paper with a spiral binding at the top. Besides my toothbrush and an old paperback copy of *The Wizard of Oz* that Mrs. Mead had scored for me at a garage sale, it was my only personal. It had to be small, due to the fact that Granny regularly tossed out the little room I slept in at the top of the stairs, looking for I don't know what. Usually, I left it in the tree house for safekeeping.

Homer said I should collect evidence, like a scientist, to figure out just where my mom was and to prove she was doing her best to find me. There wasn't a lot in my notebook, but there was enough.

One time, for instance, I heard Granny say, "No, I will not accept . . . not from that party!" And then the phone was slammed down. Beau says only way a con or conette can call out from prison is collect. Said it might very well have been Mary Bell looking to connect.

Or another thing I put in my notepad was the day I ear hustled on Sink and Dip as they talked about a lady who'd been by the house while I was at school.

"Said she was just a friend, looking in on her. Since when does Harry Sue have friends with dragon tattoos?"

What I held out for was something real: an envelope with a stamp, maybe a colored square one postmarked just before my birthday. My pudding heart hoped that if Mary Bell couldn't connect with her baby girl by telephone, she would still try to write me some letters.

I admit that what I had in my notepad didn't add up to much. But like Homer says, "Even crumbs look good to a starving man, Harry Sue."

I let him say things like that because, in a very deep way, Homer knew just exactly what I was going through. He still had a mom to fuss over him, but other than that, Homer had lost just about everything else that mattered.

Chapter 7

Planning his tree house was about the only thing that kept Homer alive in the year following his accident. You can bet it was a pretty big design challenge. He needed a fully equipped hospital bed complete with an emergency alert system and a control panel for all the functions. Since Homer was alone most of the time, he had to be the one to operate it. All he had was a head and shoulders, a chin, and a tongue.

Every morning when the weather was fine, Mrs. Dinkins or Beau or some other home health aide from the county would lower the bed on a hydraulic lift and strap Homer in. They'd pin the emergency alert button onto his T-shirt so he could just reach it if he stuck out his jaw. If you want to know what I mean, stick your bottom lip out as far as you can until your bottom teeth are in front of your top lip. Then push your chin down. That far away was where they put the alert button. Otherwise, Homer would set it off when he coughed or yawned.

With the flip of a switch, that bed was raised up, up, up, until it clicked into place in Homer's tree house. It looked just like a tree house, too, except for the bed. Mrs. Dinkins wanted to decorate, use a ladder to climb up there and put some calendar pictures on the wall from her Heavenly Highways AAA calendar. Glossy places like the Grand Canyon and Yosemite National Park, but Homer would have none of it. Busters, monkeys, T-Jones, rats—none of that in Homer's tree house. That's why he made it so if you couldn't climb the rope, you couldn't visit.

It's a wonder Mrs. Dinkins didn't build herself a home gym and start yokin' up, but even she has a teaspoon full of sense.

The bed was directly under the picture window, the one I was regularly recruited to keep free of bird poop and wet leaves and even the occasional flattened spider or nestling. Homer thought of the window as the viewing deck of a spaceship and he didn't appreciate me, his captain at arms, letting my duties slide.

He always knew I was coming before my head

popped through the hatch because the rope creaked on its metal hinge like the bellpull in a vampire movie.

And I knew as soon as I pushed open the hatch that it was without a doubt a bad day. I knew because I could smell Homer's tears. At least to me, they smell like hot pavement after rain. And I knew because his bed was flat and not raised.

"Harry Sue," he said in a whisper as I came up to the bed. "I think it's gonna rain tomorrow."

As a rule, I don't touch anyone. My heart, as you know, is in boot camp. But since Homer can't feel me, I figure touching him is the same as touching a statue or maybe better yet a tree since that, too, is a living thing that can't feel, and I don't have any special rules against touching trees. I stood up and took his hand. It was so cold that I started rubbing it. And then I brushed his hair out of his eyes. Yes, he could feel my fingers there, but would you have left a damp red-and-brown curl tickling at his eye and him with no defense but an eyelid against it?

"Let me get 'Metamorphosis,'" I said quietly, reaching for the book we were reading.

It was about a guy named Gregor Samsa and how one morning he woke up to find he'd been turned into a cockroach. Just like that. One day he was a man working some boring job trying to sell pieces of fabric and the next day . . . cockroach.

Homer thought that was funny. But he felt for the guy, too, you know?

"I wish I could get him a bed like this right next to mine," he said, "so we could be cockroaches together."

I never answered statements like that, just kept quiet, looking down at Homer.

I wish teachers would test you on the things that were most important. I want Ms. Lanier to test me on Homer's face. He had the lightest sprinkle of sand-colored freckles across the top of his nose and the same golden sand flecks in his green eyes. His mother called them hazel, but she didn't know what she was on about. They were green. Not bright green, like Magic Markers or the first leaves of spring, but an old green, like tall grass in August or dry moss on the edge of the woods. His hair was always shining with loose red-brown curls. When the sun came through the skylight, those little bits of burnt red danced all over his face, in his eyelashes and his eyebrows.

I could make a profession out of studying Homer's face. I just could. But today, it was too hard to look, as his eyes were full to spilling over and he was biting his lip to keep the sound inside.

"No," he said, letting his breath out. "It's a bad day, Harry Sue."

Of course it was, I thought as I saw the salt trails leading from his eyes to his ears.

Take the cotton out of your ears, Fish. I feel a teachable moment coming on. Remember it: Cons don't hear crying.

Of course they cry; wouldn't you? Everybody cries, Beau says, especially at night, when you're thinking about your mama and how bad you hurt her. But no con will admit to hearing it. Not if he's your road dog.

"Want me to . . . ?"

Homer nodded and turned his head while I found the Kleenex box tucked into the metal rail and pulled out a tissue. I wrapped it around my finger and stuck it in Homer's ear where his tears always ran and plugged up his ear canal so he could barely hear.

On days like these, it seemed like Homer was on the edge of something, like he was starting to fall. He was just at that moment where he was about to lose his balance. I felt so nervous, not knowing whether I would be able to catch him, to save him.

Of course, I'm not talking about falling for real. It was more like a hole of sadness he was balancing on the edge of, a sadness that could swallow him up for days.

Beau says the real name for it is special handling unit, or SHU. Don't say the letters; say, "Shoe." It's isolation, you little minnows. No people. No noise. No light. Crazy maker. But cons and conettes have their own name for it. They call it the hole.

Every once in a while, I could save Homer from the hole by grabbing him, not his body, but his mind, with an idea.

"Homer," I said, trying not to, but sounding desperate anyway. "I need a favor. Remember Violet, that lousy cheese eater who can't do her own time? She disrespected me in a major way, Homes, and I need to lay it down."

But my words were going nowhere. They were just puffs of air that came out of my mouth, just sound, like the traffic in the street below. I wasn't judging it right at all. Homer had already lost his balance.

Part 2
Falling

Some of the Monkeys seized the Tin Woodman and carried him through the air until they were over a country thickly covered with sharp rocks. Here they dropped the poor Woodman, who fell a great distance to the rocks, where he lay so battered and dented that he could neither move nor groan.

—*The Wizard of Oz*

Chapter *8*

I knew right then something that might work, but I sure hated to do it. Homer wouldn't make me if he could help it. Cons hate to go back to the scene of the crime. Nobody wants to relive it.

"Okay," I said. "It's gonna be okay, Homer. Let me get the file." I pressed the Kleenex to his face until he stopped leaking and reached under the mattress to pull out a file thick with yellowed news clippings.

Somewhere in this mess was the two-inch clipping about the Marshfield boy who'd broken his neck diving off the Grand Haven pier. But the bulk of the file, which his mother had dutifully clipped and collected at the urging of her young son, was about me, Harry Sue, the little girl who'd survived being thrown from a seventh-floor window.

I sifted through the pile to find Homer's favorite clips, not the ones that described what happened— the who, what, when, where, how—but the ones that in the weeks following the tragedy analyzed what had happened from every possible angle.

"This one's from the *Ottawa County Courier*," I said, my voice still shaking.

"LeDeaux," Homer whispered, his voice hoarse. "The scientist."

I took the cup of water from the holder at the side of the bed and put the straw in front of his lips, just barely touching. There was an important differ- ence between the way his mom did it—parting his lips with the straw like he was a baby—and the way I did. Mine was a question: "You sound hoarse. You want to drink something?" Hers was a decision: "My baby needs a drink."

Homer lifted his head, drank from the straw, and dropped it again.

"'Girl Survives Ninety-Foot Drop,' by Pierre LeDeaux. A five-year-old girl has lived to someday tell the story of how she survived a fall from the seventh floor of Destiny Towers.

"'The statistics are rather clear,' said Dr. Omar Melendez, chief of the emergency trauma unit at Ottawa County General. 'Without extenuating cir- cumstances, such as a parachute, we have no data on the survival of individuals from drops above the seventh floor. Less than two percent of individuals survive drops from the seventh floor. By the fifth floor, your rate of survival increases to fifty percent, and most will survive a drop from the second floor as long as they don't fall headfirst.'

"'The child's survival is attributed to a combination of factors,' said First Response Team Leader, fireman Harper Rowell.

"'You got rain, rain, rain, for three weeks. Heavy tree cover. Mulch. Go figure. If you'd dropped a watermelon from that high up, it's not hard to imagine what would have happened.'

"But survive she did. Little Harriet Clotkin will be a noteworthy addition to the record books. . . ."

"Notice how he never says it," Homer whispered. "He never says the word."

I knew the word he meant. But for now I held it inside, like a winning card, tight against my chest.

Homer was trying. I could see it. But he was like the Scarecrow after the winged monkeys had done their work on him. All the stuffing pulled out of him, his legs in one tree, his arms scattered across the ground.

Let me fall again if it keeps him out of the hole, I thought. *What difference does it make?*

The words I read were the straw putting him back together. One word in particular worked magic on Homer. But it wasn't time to say it yet. We were both keeping it with us in silence. Letting the tension build.

"Peter Ricci," he said now. "Luck and chance."

I pawed through the papers, dropping the folder to the floor once I'd found the clipping.

"'Young Girl Lucky to Be Alive,'" I read. "Peter Ricci in the *Spring Lake Standard*." I glanced up at Homer. His face was turned toward me. You have no idea what that meant. It was the smallest of hopeful gestures for him to turn toward me as I read, instead of facing the other plywood wall.

My heart seized up, but I looked back down quickly. I didn't smile. The thing to do was to keep reading.

"Young Harriet Clotkin is recovering from bruises, a dislocated shoulder, and two broken ribs after an argument between her parents nearly caused her death."

I always paused at this point in the article, wanting to ask this Peter Ricci: What are you saying about my mom? You think she had something to do with this?

"Initially, Garnett Clotkin dangled his daughter out the window by one leg," I forced myself to keep reading. "A drop from this position would have meant certain death. But she survives today because of a hard toss, a nearby elm, and a pile of mulch."

"See how he says that," Homer said, lifting his

head off the pillow. "It's like he's practically saying life's a crapshoot. He can't believe it, you not dying."

Now I knew it was working. Homer's neck was stretched as far forward as it could go. If his hands were up to the task, he'd be pulling himself up.

Time for Mona Sears in the *Grand Haven Gazette*. I fanned the clippings out with my foot and grabbed the article.

"In the wake of a media onslaught," I read breathlessly, "the residents of Destiny Towers are fighting to keep a reputation for violence and hard living at bay by refusing to comment on the recent near-death experience of a five-year-old girl. However, they all called the child's survival from a ninety-foot fall a"—I glanced up at Homer. His eyes were shining as he mouthed the word—"a miracle as they hurried through the courtyard to their destinations.

"'I've seen some amazing things,' said Dr. Omar Melendez, chief of the emergency trauma unit at Ottawa County General, 'but this tops them all.'

"'Sometimes there is no explanation,' said Borne Peterson, a physician at the West Michigan Clinic for Rehabilitative Services. 'In this case, there was something to break the fall.' Peterson recalled treating a man who'd fallen through a hundred-foot canopy of leaves and lived. 'Trees can absorb energy, slowing a fall,' he said.

"'As a physician, I believe in miracles. I have seen life defy science. I would say this is a very special girl.'"

"Wait a minute," Homer said, straining so hard that he caused one arm to slip through the bars of the bed and dangle at his side. "Read that last part again."

"'As a physician, I believe in miracles,'" I read, rather dramatically, to play to the audience. "'This is a very special—'"

"No, before that. About the energy."

I searched backward and found the word. "'Trees can absorb energy, slowing a fall.'"

"Amazing."

I could see it now. He was pulling himself out in one swift motion. Homer bit at his control box, making the bed rise.

"You know what that means?" he asked, eyes wide.

I stood up. I didn't have the faintest idea, but I wanted to be ready.

"That rock. At the pier. The one I hit . . ." Homer locked onto me. He could do that, grab you with his eyes, I swear, all desperate and pleading and dangerous.

"That rock at the pier. It has my energy."

You probably wouldn't understand the importance of a statement like that. I know I didn't.

"Huh? The rock?"

"Nothing," Homer said, but he had a wild look in his eyes as he stared out his window. A faraway look.

"Violet," he said finally. "She the one who always PCs up? The cheese eater with the allergies?"

I could see that he was not ready to let me in on it.

"Yeah, the one who can't do her own time."

"That's easy," Homer said, and in less than three minutes he had a plan he was sure would make Violet Chump very sorry she had dropped a dime on Harry Sue.

"You sure about this?" I asked him. "Doesn't seem like chalk can do much damage."

Homer gave me his look that said: *Who's the inventor here?*

"Before you go, I want you to set me up with my encyclopedia, Harry Sue. I want to learn more about rocks."

Using Homer's instructions, I'd mounted a little book stand on one of those trays with legs, the kind you see in movies where fake people are making breakfast in bed for their kids when they're sick. If I fit the tray under his neck just right, he could rest his chin on whatever book was on the stand and turn the pages.

I left him like that, studying rocks of all kinds, using the two-volume family encyclopedia Mrs. Dinkins had scored at a garage sale. His mind had latched on to something. Homer chewed an idea the same way Ivan Denisovich chewed his crust of bread or his little piece of potato in the book we read about him surviving life in a Russian prison. He chewed it slowly, over and over and over, until there was nothing left of it. They gave the prisoners so little bread that most of them starved to death, but the way Ivan Denisovich chewed kept him alive. By chewing that way, he wrestled every little bit of nutrition out of that piece of bread.

That's how Homer was with a new idea. If you could see it, it would look like one of those bug carcasses that pile up under a spiderweb: sucked dry.

I can't say exactly why, but as I closed the trapdoor and swung with one hand onto the knotted rope, I felt a little stab of worry about it.

Until I told myself that Harry Sue does not get intimidated by a rock.

Chapter 9

My morning chores looked like this:

1. Swipe a box of chalk from Granny's supply closet.
2. Scare Sink and Dip out of drugging the crumb snatchers.
3. Give the new art teacher the infamous Harry Sue welcome.
4. *Keep Spooner out of the muck!*

And that was all before lunch.

Let me explain. The chalk was an ingredient for revenge. It was to help teach Violet Chump a few pointers about doing her own time. Second, somebody had to make Sink and Dip realize they would be sent up if they hurt one of the babies. And every new teacher had to be educated about my bad-to-the-bone character. How else was I going to get to the joint?

The Spooner situation is a little harder to explain. Spooner's parents worked the graveyard shift at West Olive Tool and Die, which meant he got dropped off around the time we went to bed and left for home about the time I went to school. That didn't give us too much quality time together, unless you count the four times a week he woke up crying from bad dreams and I had to get him back to sleep.

His parents seemed okay. They drove a nice car. They were clean. But you don't get chased by bad dogs half the night on one of those happy TV-family shows. And then there was the little habit he had of sinking himself in the pond out back up to his eyeballs every morning just before they came to pick him up.

In our war of words, Granny called her back-yard a wetland, a unique learning opportunity. I called it a swamp. Our whole neighborhood bordered the spongy, marshy muck. The only good thing about it was it gave Homer all kinds of things to see through his window. Every once in a while a blue heron would fly through the patch of sky that was his viewing screen. He saw hawks and kestrels and turkey vultures there, too.

There's just a lot to eat in a swamp. It's like a regular bird buffet.

I gave Ferdinand Ponce de León Parker the name Spooner because of the way he backed himself right up next to my chest when I comforted him as a baby. Now that he was older, I made him stay in his own bed. Mostly that meant I spent part of the night on the braided rug next to it, holding his hand and telling him stories so he would fall back asleep.

I know what you're thinking. This is not the sort of behavior you associate with criminals.

I know that.

I always told myself that, somehow, I'd be tougher in the morning.

Spooner was the one who got me in the habit of wandering the house late at night. When he finally fell into a restless sleep, I was as wide awake as Dorothy when she first eyeballed the giant head of the Wizard of Oz.

Spooner figures into Homer's web of all things. Because he kept me up at night, I started messing with the people in China Country who were locked away in Granny's curio cabinet. To do that, I had to figure out how to pick the lock. But time goes slower from 2 to 4 a.m. For real. I can pick just about anything now with a jumbo paper clip.

I started putting the squirrel next to the princess instead of his nut. I took the kissing cousins and turned them around so their butts touched instead of their lips. Since Granny made Sink or Dip dust the cabinet a couple of times a week, she always blamed it on them.

Then later, just before the end, I started breaking off tiny little pieces, the flip of a dress or one little stuck-out princess finger. Whoever noticed the damage—Sink or Dip—would show it to the other in a panic. And if I happened to be around, I'd say casually, but loud enough for Granny to hear, "Oh, that must have been my celestial beings getting knocked out of orbit after Granny put Princella in the closet for coloring on her Quick Pick."

Or some such.

But I'm getting ahead of myself. Unless you kept him under constant surveillance, Spooner would slip outside and wade into the marsh just before his parents were due to arrive.

That morning, I used my trusty jumbo clip to pick the lock on the cheap metal cabinet where Granny kept the art supplies. She never used them herself, as I have already demonstrated. It was just a front for the parents, swung open wide during interviews to con them into believing we gave a regular course in art education.

Next, I had the challenge of keeping an eye on Spooner while grinding the chalk in the blender according to Homer's instructions.

"Special treat today," I said, picking the lock on Granny's private pantry. "We got Frosted

Flakes." My hope was that real Frosted Flakes would keep Spooner at the table.

I eyeballed the morning crowd: four sleepy crumb snatchers whose parents all worked the third shift.

Spooner looked back at me through one squinted eye.

I returned his look with my look that said: *Please don't burn the spot, Spooner.*

I had too many other things to do.

"Spooner's gonna pour," I said.

The crumb snatchers on the graveyard shift knew the drill. Keep quiet and eat your chow. Granny didn't allow for much noise before 9 a.m.

Too bad I wasn't one of them.

I dumped the chalk in the blender and pressed the button. Clouds of white dust spewed out of the top. I let it run until I couldn't take the burned smell of the motor any longer. Then I poured it all in a paper bag and tossed it in my backpack.

As soon as I turned around, I realized my "please don't burn the spot" look did not have the desired effect. Spooner had flown.

Dang.

I glanced at the rest of the crumb snatchers and then back at the clock. I'd have to work fast. There was plenty of danger for three sleepy preschoolers in Granny's kitchen and I refused to risk it. I pulled the box of matches off the window ledge and ran upstairs and down the hall until I stood right under the smoke alarm. I lit a match, blew it out, and let smoke drift upward. It's what I call "Granny's little alarm clock."

As a rule, I didn't like to rely on Granny to oversee the crumb snatchers. But she'd have to do in a pinch.

I ran back downstairs, aimed cereal at three bowls, splashed on milk, tossed a handful of plastic spoons on the table, and took off after Spooner.

"I am not gettin' dirty today," I yelled into the marsh grass and duckweed at the end of the backyard. Pretty soon I heard the sound of water sucking into mud.

"Dang it, Spooner." I pulled off my shoes and socks and rolled up my jeans.

"Okay, okay, look. I'm a stupid zebra coming down here all by myself for a drink of water." I waded in. The grass could cut you like glass if you weren't careful. And man, was it cold.

See, Spooner's mom was from Spain and his dad was from Portland, which made him exactly . . . a crocodile. Spooner loved crocodiles. It was the only way to get through to the kid. Call him an alligator and he won't look you in the eye for days.

"Crocodiles love zebras," I said, wading up to my knees and watching the stink water soak into the rolled-up fabric of my jeans. I parted a clump of grass shot through with old stalks of purple loose-strife and was picking seedpods out of my hair when he sprang at me.

Little bits of algae and swamp muck spattered my shirt. A crayfish clamped on to my sleeve.

"Awww," I screamed in a miserable way as he pawed at me. "Right on my muzzle. I'm a goner."

I wrestled the skinny little bit of nothing that was Spooner soaking wet onto land.

"Now you're gonna shake me and shake me until my arms and legs fly off and I'm nothing but a zebra burrito."

I dragged him back to the house, swamp stink clinging to my skin. Spooner wasn't giving up any information. Of all the crumb snatchers at Granny's Lap, Spooner and Hammer Head had my vote for "most likely to survive the joint." Hammer Head because he'd scare the pants off all but the most experienced cons. And Spooner because he didn't mind funky. Not one bit. That, and he seemed to me like a serious candidate for the ding wing.

Chapter 10

Granny was glaring at me from the window, a peppermint stick clamped between her teeth—no cigars until the graveyard shift had been picked up. I splashed cold water from the outdoor tap onto me and Spooner, hoping it would rinse out enough of the smell so I wouldn't attract attention. At least so Ms. Lanier wouldn't spray me with that fruit stuff. Harry Sue does not wear foo foo.

"What the bee-jeezus happened here?" Granny asked, swiping at the chalk on the counter and grinding peppermint between her teeth. She still had on her pink shower cap, the one that covered all the pin curlers. Her red-rimmed eyes and naked lids hadn't been painted and plastered over with makeup yet, so she looked like one of those pink hairless laboratory rats.

Sink looked up from the table, where she'd joined the kids.

"What is that stuff?" she asked me, knowing full well I wouldn't answer to Granny.

"That?" I plastered Spooner into his chair and slid a bowl over to him. "Why, that's cocaine," I told her.

Sink rolled her eyes and began picking glumly at the dried-up bits of cereal on the table. Dip moved from her place in the doorway to a seat at the table and pulled the box of cereal toward her, pouring for Spooner and herself.

Everyone used slow, deliberate movements in the morning to avoid getting a clout from Granny. They knew it was lockdown until she'd had two cups of coffee.

"I'm gonna give it to the kids to keep 'em happy all day long," I said, loud enough for Granny to hear. Truth to tell, Granny was more than a little deaf, and the extra noise made everybody at the table jump.

"See, I was gonna use cold medicine," I kept on, calmly patting myself with paper towels, "but yesterday at school, I saw on the Internet how this lady down in Florida got sent up for an eight ball for accidentally killing a baby she was trying to keep quiet."

"You're a liar," Dip said, pinching a big fold of her bloated cheek.

I yanked the wax bag of cereal out of the Frosted Flakes box.

"Eight years and change . . ."

I stopped then, knowing I had everybody's ear, even the pink rat slurping coffee at the counter. Reaching into the junk drawer for a bottle of Elmer's glue, I put two big blobs on the counter and smacked the empty Frosted Flakes box over them. About twice a year, Granny bought some nice name-brand cereal and let the kids eat it. For days afterward, she left the empty box on the counter for show.

"Perfect," I said, leaning back to admire my work, "for seeing when you walk in the door to pick up your kids."

Spooner stretched in his seat to get a look at what I was doing and accidentally knocked over the milk pitcher; what was left ran lazily to the edge of the table and started dripping on the floor. Granny was at him in a hot minute. She had a plastic spatula in her hand, and if I knew Granny, she was going to plant a few on the back of his head.

But I was too quick for her. I yanked it out of her hand and pointed it at Sink and Dip.

"www dot . . ." I jabbed the spatula in their direction.

They both ducked. I could be as lousy as Granny

if I wanted to. *"www.angelsbeforetheirtime.com,"* I said, taking a deep breath in. "Eight years and change. Think about it. No perfume. No boys. No sleeping in."

I grabbed my backpack, the one I'd had for the last four years, the one with the duct tape on the bottom to keep the guts from falling out, and paused in front of Serendipity.

"Imagine a bright orange jumpsuit with 'Dip' embroidered on the pocket," I said.

Though the girls tried to act like nothing I said bothered them in the least, Dip had to shudder when I mentioned the color orange.

Orange was a fall color, see? And whenever she worked up the colors that looked best on her, Dip was a summer every time.

I heard tires crunching on gravel and watched Granny disappear, swearing under her breath, to get her company robe. I decided not to stay for the charade.

"Have a loving and licensed day, all," I said, and I was out the door.

Glancing at the clock on my way out, I figured it would be a miracle if I made it to school before Ms. Lanier, as I'd planned.

Which got me started on miracles again.

"Do you believe in miracles?" Homer asked on his bad days. Since Mom went down, I got so good at lying, I could lie to my own self and believe it.

But I couldn't lie to Homer.

Only one thing has ever happened to me that could be described as a miracle, but I suppose I sided with the policeman quoted in one of those articles Homer had me read to him over and over again.

"If you look at it in a certain way, little Harriet was mighty lucky."

I burned through a lot of luck on that flight.

I keep hoping I didn't burn through it all.

I don't know why Homer was so endlessly fascinated with my fall. Was it because he jumped a fraction of the distance and things ended up so badly? Maybe it's just that, as he puts it, I flew in the face of reason. And that puzzles him.

For most people it's forgotten history. What the old teachers at Trench Vista Elementary tell the new ones is that my father threw me out the window. Or they say I survived a ninety-foot fall. Mom doesn't get much play in either version.

She was an addict, I know, but she was addicted to good things, too. Like me, for instance. Like books.

I remember sliding my hands over the stacks of glossy-covered library books that filled our arms as we rode home on the bus. I remember her reading to me late in the night on her days off, lying in bed, trying to ease me into sleep. My mom could be doing laundry, painting her nails, talking on the phone, but if I wobbled over to her with a book in my hand, she'd pull me onto her lap and we'd read it.

She liked fairy tales best, liked getting lost in the pictures. We went east of the sun and west of the moon, more north than north, more south than south.

And she had a powerful urge to know, not just the stories but the authors, too. She liked to talk back to them, tell them to lighten up some or change a scene to suit her way of thinking.

"They're mysterious ones, Harry Sue," she said, combing her fingers down the back of my head. "How else could they know everybody's secrets?"

That's when she informed me of the little-known fact that the *L* in L. Frank Baum stood for Louise.

"Boy name and a girl name, just like you," she said, poking me in the gut. "I bet you're gonna be a big famous writer someday, too.

"Just do me one favor, baby, okay? Don't make it so hard for the heroes to find their way home."

When things got real bad for the peasant girl, the one who couldn't sleep until she reached the castle and had to prop herself up in the trees with wolves howling around, Mom cried. Or the prince who couldn't make a sound when he was attacked by demons and kicked and punched and stung and bit . . . that just tore her up.

Some teachers don't want to read that stuff to

kids because they think it'll give 'em bad dreams. But I could tell them real stories that would curl their hair. Even Louise Frank Baum got mixed up in all that when he wrote at the beginning to *The Wizard of Oz* that he didn't want his book to be like the crummy old tales that scare kids with beasts and demons.

What he said was—straight up, Fish! I copied this out of the book—what he said was this: "The modern child seeks only entertainment in its wonder tales and gladly dispenses with all disagreeable incident."

He said that's why he wrote *The Wizard of Oz*, because he wanted a story "in which the wonderment and joy are retained and the heart-aches and nightmares are left out."

Either that guy had a real sense of humor or he had no respect for the power of his words. Do you even know the real story of how the Tin Man got to be the way he did? He started out a man, a poor woodcutter who fell in love with a pretty Munchkin girl. But that girl served an old woman who didn't want her to get married and leave, so the old woman promised a sheep and a cow to the Wicked Witch of the East if she'd stop it from happening. The witch cast a spell on the woodcutter's ax and it chopped off his leg. He was down about that, you know, but he found a tinsmith to put a tin leg on for him and then he was good to go. Well, that didn't set too well with the witch, so she bewitched the ax again.

You get the picture. Over and over. A leg. An arm. His chest. His head. The ax cut it all off. And piece by piece the tinsmith replaced real flesh and blood with tin.

Now, I don't know about you. But that doesn't seem like a sweet little bedtime story to me.

I mean, seriously, Fish, what kind of tea was that guy drinking?

Chapter 11

As I padded down the silent halls of Trench Vista Elementary, I realized that I must have a little luck left in my share because today was Friday. I'd forgotten about Mr. Hernandez's team meetings, where he called the teachers together before school on Friday to "assess" in his office.

Every classroom was open and empty and as vulnerable as a sleeping con. I could be very efficient under the circumstances. First I spent a little quality time marinating Ms. Lanier's erasers in the chalk dust I brought from Granny's.

Then I went looking for the art room. Our newest teacher was replacing a mousy little something just out of college who claimed the moldy air at Trench Vista gave her the shingles. Even though I don't have a lot of good things to say about the air around here, it seemed to me like life was what gave Miss Rodenski the shingles.

Miss Rodenski kept her room and her supplies in perfect order and seemed disappointed when the students had to use them for the day's lessons. After the kids filed out, she worked feverishly on the last bit of dried-on glue or splotch of paint before the next class came in. If we got there before she had the room to her satisfaction, she'd make us wait in the hall while she stayed inside scrubbing and cursing the cleaning gods. All that cursing and cleaning didn't set too well with Mr. Hernandez.

The room was just as Miss Rodenski left it, looking like a picture out of a magazine: paint lined up on low shelves according to the color wheel, brushes stored tip up, markers stored tip down, colored pencils boxed and sharpened to a lethal point.

I walked over to the desk. It was clean except for Miss Rodenski's planner and a wooden carving of a hand with hinges at the fingers so you could pose it any old which way. It called to mind the Tin Man again and I ran my hands over the smooth palm, pressing each wooden finger to it, making a fist.

As I stood there, I noticed a strange hot smell I couldn't put a name to. I rattled the drawers, but they were locked. The smell, like spices and hot, hot sunshine, made me want to pick the lock and get at whatever it was. But I wasn't here for that.

My stomach rebelled as I turned away. I still hadn't eaten even one handful of the Frosted Flakes I'd scored off Granny.

I checked the planner and saw that the new teacher had a bunch of kindergarten crumb snatchers first period. I glanced around, trying to figure the best way to shoot to the bottom of her list.

The new teacher was a substitute, Mr. Hernandez told us, just working out the rest of the year until a real art teacher could be found. But that didn't matter to me. I had a reputation to uphold and substitutes were easier than most to mess with.

Every new teacher needed my welcome-wagon treatment. It laid the foundation for my bad-to-the-bone character assessments. Every once in a while, somebody would catch me helping a crumb snatcher who'd fallen off the slide or busting up a fight so that nobody got hurt, and they'd think there was a little promise in the old girl. That's when I had to hit back hard. Where it counted.

With Miss Rodenski, it was easy. I just messed up her supplies. But I've also staged gladiator fights for Mr. Hernandez, snipped the tails off Mr. Pandowdy's collection of snake skins, and put a stink bomb in Ms. Meyering's coat closet to return my rep to lower-than-curbside Trench Vista trash.

Homer was the clever one, with his concoctions

and inventions. Me, I was low-tech. I either broke stuff or mad-dogged the teachers. When I saw the finger paints set next to the cookie sheets in their nice little squeeze bottles, I scooped them all up and headed for the sink.

Carefully, I squirted half of each bottle down the drain before topping it off with water. That would make a nice mess when the crumb snatchers aimed their bottles at a cookie sheet. I even had a little fun while I was at it, seeing as I rarely got to art class due to certain restrictions Mr. Hernandez had placed on my movement.

The last bottle I fixed was purple. Instead of shooting it at the drain, I aimed for the bottom of the stainless steel sink and used my finger to swirl it around. Just for a minute. I didn't try to make anything, just enjoyed the way my finger felt in the cool paste. Like a blob of purple pudding. I pushed it round and round in a circle.

"Even though I am a grown man, I still myself enjoy painting with my fingers."

I whirled around. In front of me stood a very tall man with skin so dark it was the color of blue midnight.

"Allow me to introduce myself. I am Mr. Olatanju. Your new art teacher."

"Harry Sue," I mumbled, looking at the floor and swiping my hands on my shirt.

"Harry Sue," he said slowly. His voice was

strange and deep, pronouncing each word carefully, just a little different than it was supposed to sound. Instead of "Harry" with a "hair" in it, he said, "Har-ee."

I almost forgot to glare.

"Isn't that a boy's name? Har-ee?"

"So?" I said, conjuring up *mad and dumb*.

Mr. Olatanju said nothing. He looked at me as if I were a puzzle that he did not know how to figure. He held his chin in his hand.

I wasn't used to people looking at me directly, but I forced myself to lock into his stare.

"In my handbook, it is clear that I must never touch a student, particularly if we are alone in the room. Since it is my first day, Har-ee Sue, I will not put my hands on your shoulders to see if they are as uneven as they look to me now."

He pulled a chair up and, twirling it around, sat on it backward, his elbows on the chair back, considering me. I noticed how high his knees reached when he was sitting, almost to his shoulders.

"My wife is a healer. She could help you with the pain."

I resisted the urge to knead my shoulder—which was aching—and give him the satisfaction. It was making more sense now. What with the funny way he talked and his dark, dark skin, this hack was from faraway Africa. I'd seen pictures in

National Geographic of those voodoo ladies, all naked sagging boobs with rings around their necks.

No voodoo lady was gonna lay a hand on Harry Sue.

"You gonna give me detention?"

Mr. Olatanju gave me a puzzled look.

"You know, punish me for messing up your stuff."

"Punish you?" he asked, still peering at me. "For finger painting?"

Chapter *12*

After I gave the guy several good reasons to punish me—note that most teachers don't need help in that department—I went outside to line up for the day. I made sure to give Violet a big smile before I took my place behind her. She wrinkled her nose and turned to face forward. *Yeah, yeah.* I knew I still smelled from the morning.

I wished I had some of that stuff from the art guy's desk, the stuff that smelled like hot and sun, so that I would not smell like swamp and dead things. But I told myself that the joint would smell a lot worse. I had to get used to funky 24-7.

I was just standing there in line, trying to figure out what happened in the art room, when I felt a hard pinch right between my shoulder blades. Somebody was pulling on my shirt.

"Told you," said Jolly Roger Chlorine loudly.

I chose not to turn around.

"She doesn't wear one. Or should I say *it* doesn't wear one."

Now *that* demanded attention. Nobody disrespects Harry Sue and gets away with it.

I turned around to face Jolly Roger Chlorine, which was the nick I gave him because he has the conscience of a bloodthirsty pirate *and* a patch of hair so white it looks bleached. Maybe this morning wouldn't be a waste of time, after all. I hoped Mr. Africa was looking out the window.

"Jolly Roger," I said calmly. "I didn't know you had an interest in ladies' underwear." There was a fit of laughter and shoulder punching by Roger's crew.

"But since you asked, I'll tell you. I do have one, but it was under so much strain that it broke, see? And I had to order the replacement parts from the Victoria's Secret catalog."

Course everybody knows about Victoria's Secret 'cause the catalog got passed around the school plenty before Mr. Hernandez confiscated it.

Roger glared at me.

I gave him my look that said: *Mess with H.S. and live to regret it.*

He pushed my shoulders to get something started.

I pushed back.

He shoved me so hard, I fell out of line.

"I saw that, Mr. Coindine," Mr. Hernandez said. "You can come with me."

"If you're lucky, J.R., I'll let you try it on when it's all fixed up," I whispered as Mr. Hernandez took him roughly by the elbow.

One of these days, Jolly Roger and his road dogs were going to flatten me, I knew. I didn't have a crew at school, so like Homer said, I had to watch my back twice as sharp.

Homer just hated that he didn't have my back at school. I never told him about any trouble on the yard he couldn't have a hand in fixing. He had to know he was still there for me somehow, didn't he?

Beau says that when you're on the outs, you got friends who will take a hit for you, but in the joint, they just dry up and blow. Nobody comes to see you. Nobody writes.

But not everything Beau said would hang true for me. I mean, I ask you, Fish. What were my options here? Click up with Jolly Roger? Hang tough with Violet Chump?

I don't think so. Violet is what Beau calls a "buster."

Rhymes with "can't trust her."

Remember that.

Everything but one thing went just the way

Homer and I figured it would. It was during social studies, when Ms. Lanier wanted to draw a map of the United States to show where the major crops of our great country were grown, that it happened.

She tried to erase the chalkboard she used for map drawing, but all she made was big eraser prints on the board.

"I guess I need a volunteer to clap these erasers," she said.

I waved my hand in the air like I knew the answer to the million-dollar question.

"Oh! Oh! Oh!" I said. Pretty convincing, I must admit.

That got Violet's attention, because if I wanted something, she was sure to want to take it away from me. That was just Violet.

She propped her elbow on the desk and wiggled her fingers.

"Thank you, Violet," Ms. Lanier said, and held out both erasers.

Violet had no way of knowing those erasers had an entire box of chalk on them. I figured she'd take them outside for a little clap and her dress would be covered in chalk. There would be chalk in her hair, on her eyelashes, up her nose. Violet hated dirt of any kind. She would have to sit in her seat, covered from head to toe in white powder, because no matter how you try, the only thing that gets off chalk is soap and water. She would sit there, looking like a prissy ghost, and feel the way she made Harry Sue feel as the other kids giggled and pointed.

As she sat in her seat for the rest of the day, trying to disappear, I would lean over and say calmly, "Gee, Violet, looks like there was a whole box of chalk on those erasers. That's strange. They weren't like that before you disrespected Harry Sue."

And I'd give a repeat performance of my look that said: *Mess with Harry Sue and live to regret it.*

But that didn't happen.

It was in the middle of her sentence: "The Great Plains states formed the backbone of the country's grain cro—" that Ms. Lanier looked toward the door, squinted, dropped her chalk, and ran.

She didn't go anywhere at first because she always wore those pumps with shiny bottoms that aren't good for scratch. But after a couple seconds we saw her little knees pop out from her skirt and Ms. Lanier made tracks. That was such an unusual sight that the rest of us froze in our seats. It got so quiet you coulda heard a rat piss on cotton. That is, until J.R. ran to the door to eye hustle.

"Ole Violet's having a fit," he said.

Ms. Lanier nearly toppled him rushing back into the room. She threw open Violet's desk, scooping the contents onto the floor.

"Where is the inhaler?" she sobbed. *"Where is Violet's inhaler?"*

That's where I left her, scrabbling in the bottom of Violet's desk.

I shot out of the room. Nobody runs faster than Harry Sue. Violet was doubled over in the hall, her face blue, her hair white with chalk dust.

Down the hall I ran. When I got to the main office, I busted through the double doors, detoured around the secretary's desk, and swung open the door to the nurse's office. Mrs. Finster looked up from the magazine she was reading and blinked at me.

"Give me Violet Chump's rescue inhaler," I managed to croak out.

Mrs. Finster straightened her nurse's cap and reached into the file drawer of her metal desk.

"Now Harry Sue," she said, beginning to push herself up from the chair with the inhaler in her left hand. "You know I can't just give you someone else's—"

As soon as I could get a clear grab, I snatched it. "You better call an ambulance," I shouted back as I took off running once again.

Ms. Lanier was trying to get Violet to sit up when I returned. Her legs were twitching all over the place. Her dress was bunched up around her waist.

Without waiting for instructions, I shoved the inhaler in her mouth and pressed hard. Violet sucked on it greedily, making little sobbing noises until her eyes stopped looking like a cornered chipmunk's. Ms. Lanier tried to hold her still and pull the hair back off her face. The ambulance men came clattering down the hall and pushed me aside, pressing a plastic oxygen mask to Violet's mouth.

When it looked like Violet was out of the woods, Ms. Lanier grabbed me from behind and started to cry.

"Thank you, Harry Sue. I don't know what happened in there. I lost my head for a minute."

She pulled my chin up and gave me a peck on the cheek. Then she sat down next to me and Violet and rubbed her eyes, smearing mascara all over them. Then Ms. Lanier looked at me as if I were someone else. The look she gave me was not in her normal catalog of looks.

Violet, who'd been clenching both my wrists in her hands while she was choking, gave me a funny look, too.

Mr. Hernandez came rushing down the hall, followed by Mrs. Finster. "Ms. Lanier! What is happening here?"

"Harry Sue just saved Violet's life is what's happening here," she declared proudly.

I shrank back. This was the part Homer and I had not predicted. I mean, if I'd sat in my seat and let old Violet find her eternal reward, they'd be clapping me in handcuffs right now instead of looking at me all googly-eyed.

Why couldn't I be more like Dorothy?

She wastes two witches without even trying and doesn't lose sleep over it.

I couldn't even do an accident right.

Chapter *13*

My weak heart did a couple of flip-flops be-fore I thought of something to keep the day from being an entire loss.

"Mr. Hernandez," I said, "I might as well tell you, I messed up that new art teacher's room. Yeah, that was me. I wrecked his project."

Mr. Hernandez gazed at me over his skinny glasses. "You've been busy today, Harry Sue." He helped me to my feet and put his arm around my shoulders as we started walking down the hall.

"Why don't you let me get back to you on that one? It may be hard to work up enthusiasm for punishing you today, Harry Sue, seeing as you just saved Violet's life."

He patted me on the back and continued to his

office. I slid down the wall and put my head in my hands. Who else could mess up so royally?

"Maybe you could grant Mr. Olatanju some special dispensation," Mr. Hernandez added from a few feet away. "After all, he's only here until we complete our new search."

But I wasn't really listening to Mr. Hernandez anymore. I was too busy losing my balance.

In point of fact, Fish, I was already falling.

Now everyone would think of me as a hero—which was bad enough—but even worse, I had almost killed Violet. I didn't want to kill anybody. I never did. I was already responsible for one death I hadn't meant to happen. Couldn't that be enough?

Nobody was playing by the rules. A conette needs order. She needs the joint mentality. Good guys. Bad guys. Hacks. Road dogs. Fish.

I started to cry in that way I have that doesn't involve tears, just little gulps of air that swirled the muck at the bottom of my stomach.

Why didn't she write me? They'd have to tell me, wouldn't they, if she'd been paralyzed like Homer? Could she really be in lockdown these last six years? Maybe she was writing and Granny filched the letters? But how? Was she hiding them somewhere? Why would Mary Bell leave me all alone with Granny, knowing what a bad influence she was? I'd rather be in the joint, rather be locked up tight, if it meant we could be together again. And she would read to me . . . something with a happy ending so I could fall asleep, not thinking about how it had been at the end. For Garnett . . .

Homer wasn't the only one who went to the hole. I went there, too.

When you go to the SHU, it means you've done something very bad, like started a riot or knifed somebody. Think about it. What do you do to a conette who breaks the law in prison? You have to have someplace very bad to send her.

Sometimes you get a bed, sometimes not. Sometimes they make it completely dark. You can go crazy in there when it's dark for days at a time. You start talking to yourself, hearing voices. The walls close in.

A button can be your best friend. Or an ant. Throwing a button in the dark and playing hide-and-seek with it. Or feeling an ant crawl across your bare skin. It keeps your mind occupied.

I didn't want to go to the hole today.

I didn't want to be left alone with my thoughts.

So I took off running.

I ran out the side door and down a muddy path and through two neighborhoods with tight brick houses and across four busy streets without looking until I was damp with sweat and spattered with mud and there was a cramp inside that grabbed a chunk of skin and ribs and squeezed tight.

I was fighting for breath by the time I reached

Homer's tree and hauled myself up, arm over arm, without using my legs at all. I liked pain when I was on the edge of the hole. Pain helped me to balance, to concentrate. Maybe I wouldn't fall in.

"Homer," I panted, out of breath, clenching my biceps where they throbbed. My back and shoulder were on fire like always when I ran too fast.

His bed was tilted up and he stared dreamily out the window.

"The leaves have started their free fall," he said. Once the leaves were gone, Homer would have to stay all day in the house with Mrs. Dinkins for the winter.

But I didn't want to talk about the leaves.

"I need an invention to teach those juveniles to respect me," I said, gulping, running the back of my hand over my face.

"But I don't want to hurt anybody, Homes."

He turned to look at me, but I kept my eyes down, picking at the dried spots of mud on the tails of my shirt.

"You going soft, Harry Sue?"

I shook my head. "I just don't want to hurt anybody," I repeated. "I just want to do my own time."

Homer said nothing.

"Be left alone."

He nodded, waiting. But I wasn't ready to let him in on it.

"How'd it go with old Violet?"

Every once in a while a look slipped out, a desperate look that said: *Please, Homer, not now!*

And Homer turned his head to the wall, which meant: *It's okay, dog, we don't have to go there.*

"What kind of invention?"

I told Homer about Jolly Roger and what he said in the morning line regarding my female parts. How he called me "it."

"Those are fighting words, Homes," I said, trying to care about it, trying to keep my edge.

Down in the street, I heard a noise like the recycling truck ca-chunking along, then a screech of tires and silence.

Homer didn't seem to notice the commotion at all. He just stared out his window. He was concentrating. Sometimes, he said, he could will a leaf to let go with his mind. He would watch it carefully for minutes, thinking, *Jump, jump!* Until finally it couldn't take the pressure and it went, just like Homer did, leaving behind everything it knew, falling slowly toward the dark unknown.

"I got an idea that'll knock him off his feet," he said finally.

"Okay . . ."

"But we'll need some battery power."

"Where am I going to hide batteries?"

I could tell he liked the idea. I started to let myself breathe regular. Everything would be fine.

Nothing permanent happened to Violet. She was a little slow on the uptake, so less oxygen to her brain probably wouldn't cause much of a stir.

It was just me and Homer now, cooking up another plan.

"Let me think on it for a minute and I'll give you my list," he said.

I retreated to the corner closest to Homer's head and pulled out the notepad I'd tucked away under the mattress. I had nothing new to add, except this thought that occurred to me in the hall outside Ms. Lanier's room that maybe Granny had a stash of my letters from Mary Bell. It wasn't the first time it had occurred to me. Hiding a letter Mary Bell sent to me would be a worse punishment than any I could dream up, so of course Granny would do it.

But I couldn't write that down because I didn't have any evidence for it. The notepad was only for real things. Still, reading the other entries calmed me, and I held the pad in front of my face, pushing my back against the wall and sliding down until my knees were under my chin. Sometimes I just sat there, pushing my heels closer to my butt by pressing on my toes, trying to see how small a space I could take up. When I was done looking, I slipped the notepad back into its place.

Homer needed quiet to think. I tried to use my thumbnail to press my initials in the floor, but it just bent back, giving me a new pain to think about.

And that made fresh the desperate look of pain in Violet's eyes when she couldn't get any air.

So instead I stared at Homer's hand, lying still on the cover, as stiff and still as the wooden hand on Mr. Blue-midnight-art-teacher's desk. That's when I decided on my punishment for accidentally saving Violet's life.

I couldn't stroke Homer's hand today, no matter that it would be like touching a tree. Today, even touching trees was off-limits.

Chapter 14

Suddenly Homer turned to look at me in surprise, and I realized that the winch holding the rope was creaking. Just a second later, the trap door popped open and the skinny arm and head of a lady with short orange hair and hands the size of Ping-Pong paddles appeared in Homer's private space.

She stared at me with surprise but didn't say anything, just hauled herself up and took a look around. She stood there, glaring down at Homer, her long fingers twitching on his bedcover.

"Where's Beau?" Homer asked.

"Where do you think? Cooling his heels in the Cook County Correctional Facility for drawing with a knife."

There was a long silence.

"On people," she added, as if we didn't already get it.

There was a look on her face. I couldn't read it, but it bothered me. It made me push myself up so that I stood against the wall, ready, in case Homer needed me. She stood completely still, except for the twitching fingers on the bedcover.

She was wearing a turtleneck and over that a thin shapeless dress, like a sundress for a fat lady. But even all that flimsy cloth couldn't hide that she was small and tight, like she'd been twisted out of metal coat hangers.

A long slow smile spread across her face. She looked like she wanted to eat Homer.

Pulling a slip of paper out of one of the bulging front pockets of her dress, she read: "Christopher Dinkins, aka Homer Price. Quad with contingent psycho-social factors . . ."

She paused. Looked around.

"I assume that's why we're up in this tree?"

"Because I'm a quad or because I have psycho-social factors?" Homer asked, his head turned to the opposite wall.

The woman rubbed her fingers along her chin in an exaggerated way.

"I have seen quads do amazing things, but climb trees? No, that I have never seen. So it must be because you're a bit of a nut.

"A nut in a tree. I like that. A nut in a tree. That's good."

I could see she was having a bad effect on Homer, and I searched through all my tricks to think of something to throw her off balance.

"Now, if you'd be so kind as to move over, Homer. I'd like to experience the world from your point of view."

Without waiting for permission, her hands disappeared under the cover and she slid Homer to the side of the bed.

He turned to look at me, but I stayed where I was. I wanted to know what she was playing at. It wasn't safe to take her down in the tree house, anyway. Not with the bed taking up half the room.

Then her little body was under the cover with her arms down at her sides, just like Homer's. She smiled and closed her eyes.

"Just like Matisse," she said. And then she stopped talking.

We waited for her to make her point. Just like Matisse . . . because . . . *what?!*

When I thought I couldn't stand still another second, she propped her head on her hand and said to Homer: "Did you know that at the end of his life, the great painter Matisse was confined to his bed? Instead of lying there all wasted, he taped a piece of chalk to a stick and drew shapes on the ceiling."

"Then this isn't *just* like Matisse, is it?" Homer asked sharply. "Because I can't draw."

She had the nerve to move a lock of Homer's hair off his face. He looked like he might bite her for that.

"Ah, but the technology exists for you to be Matisse."

She hopped out of bed. "My name is Anna Sorenson. I have a degree in art education, am licensed in therapeutic massage, and am currently finishing up my course work at the Borne-Benson School of Chiropractic.

"But right now," she said, smiling happily, "I need to check you for bedsores."

For the second time she slid her fingers under the bedcover.

"What are you doing here?" I asked from my place against the wall.

Anna covered her mouth with her hands and backed away from the bed, her eyes wide in surprise, mocking me.

"Well, hello there," she said after a minute. "You must be the other fugitive from this game we call life. The one. The only. Harry Sue Clotkin." She stuck out her hand, real friendly.

I looked at the ground. I wasn't about to shake hands with her.

"When will Beau be back?" I asked.

"Not today. Of that we can be certain."

And as if that settled everything, Anna continued to probe Homer's body, her hands moving beneath the cover like some kind of alien. Both Homer
and I stared at them with disgust.

I mean, think about it. Sure, he couldn't feel a
thing, but wouldn't you be disgusted if some crazy
lady you never met started running her hands
south of your belly button?

Anna didn't seem to notice us at all. She looked
like she was playing an instrument, her face had
such a look of fierce concentration.

After a minute, she said, "What do we got to
work with here, Homer, my boy?"

Homer didn't answer. His look said: *Let me do
my own time.*

"Is he always this uncooperative?" Anna
asked me.

I straightened and made two fists, though I kept
my arms at my sides.

"I think you better go, Anna Sorenson," I said,
taking a step forward. "Homer doesn't want you
here."

"I think you better help," Anna said, tossing me
what looked like a tube of toothpaste from the
pocket of her dress. "Your friend here has skin like
tissue paper. It has to be protected.

"Now, Homer, I'm not going anywhere until
you answer my question. What still works?"

Homer looked right back at Anna Sorenson. He

drilled her with his eyes. Then he delivered the classic quadriplegic gesture of disrespect.

He stuck out his tongue.

What happened next is a little hard to describe. Anna Sorenson proceeded to use the metal rail on the bed like a step stool. Before we knew it, she had leapt from the top of the rail to hang from the crossbeam in the ceiling. She stuck out her tongue and wagged it back and forth. She whipped her legs around like an eggbeater. We could see right up her dress to her underwear. It was loose and white with little frilly stuff around the leg holes, like old ladies wear. Stuff was flying from her pockets: roles of adhesive, tweezers, a stethoscope, a little *Sesame Street* watch.

I was frozen in panic, sure she would fall right on top of Homer. But she didn't. She dropped to the floor and stood there, staring at us and panting. After she caught her breath, she stood up straight, put her hand on her heart, and said, just like a TV announcer:

"A tongue is a terrible thing to waste."

I knew I had to help Homer. But the bed was between us. She would see my move coming from a long way off.

"And now, Homer, for something completely different . . ." She pulled off the bedcover with a snap. "I'm gonna teach your girlfriend about flexion."

I tensed. She wasn't going to teach me anything.

"C'mon, Harold," she said, patting the bed. "Over here."

"Give me one good reason," I said.

Anna looked up at me and sighed. I was giving her my "somewhere, somehow, when you least expect it, I will exact my punishment" look, only instead of taking her breath away, like it did Violet's, she yawned.

"You two are a piece of work, you know that? Okay, how about this?"

She began talking very slowly, just the way I did when I wanted the crumb snatchers to pick something up.

"Your friend here has to stimulate his skin. Normally, at his age, he might be trying to grab a girl's behind, pinch a pack of gum, change the trucks on his skateboard, but as you can see"—she held out her big paddle hands, gesturing toward Homer's still body—"it ain't likely.

"So if we don't help along his circulation with flexing and pointing . . ."

She picked up one of Homer's arms and fell to concentrating again. There was something about the way she moved his arm, bending and stretching, bending then stretching, gentle and fluid, never exactly stopping, that made me take notice. Something was telling me that Anna Sorenson was good at what she did.

Very good.

"Without stimulation, his skin will start tearing like a bunch of your granny's old silk panty hose. Maybe it's me, but I figured that while the two of you are hiding out from the world up here, you could at least do your part to keep our Homer from tearing at the seams."

Her speech was over, but I didn't move. I wasn't at all sure what to do. I knew Homer had to be moved around so he didn't get bedsores. Think about it. He couldn't move on his own. Ever. At all. So he had to be turned like a piece of meat in a marinade or a potted plant that needs all sides to face the sun. I knew his skin had to have air.

She put me in a bad place, you know? Homer was my road dog. I couldn't let anything bad happen to him.

"When Beau came, he turned him to his side," I told her, mumbling my words to show I wasn't giving her respect.

Anna Sorenson cupped her hand behind her ear and listened to me. She looked again at Homer's body and bent real close, her nose almost touching his thigh.

"Sorry to say this, but your friend Beau is a hack."

Homer threw me a quick look. What was that supposed to mean? Hacks were guards as far as we knew. Enemies. Beau had taught us the ropes, the joint jive, the convict's code. Beau was *not* the enemy.

"Harry Sue, I'm willing to bet you're the kind of woman for whom seeing is believing," she went on. "So come and take a gander."

I looked at Homer and he nodded. I walked over to her side of the bed.

"Sure, he needs exposure to air. Skin needs that. But look at this color here."

I forced myself to look at Homer's thin legs. Atrophy. That's what it's called. When you don't use the muscles, they just fade away. His legs looked like a couple of plastic plumbing pipes lying there. Anna was pointing to a spot on his thigh that looked like a big bruise.

"That's mottling," she said. "That means there's not enough oxygen on either side, for the skin or the blood. When that happens, the skin gets stale and it dies."

Anna Sorenson replaced the cover gently and looked me up and down.

"You're strong enough, that's for certain. Otherwise you couldn't haul your skinny rear up that rope. If you weren't so crooked, you might aspire to the fine career of a home health aide yourself. But even the Hunchback of Notre Dame could push Homer here around in a wheelchair, don't you think? He can't weigh much more than a scarecrow."

Anna sat down on the bed, swinging her legs back and forth.

"I'm coming back, you know," she said. "Day after tomorrow."

She scooped her belongings together and stuffed them back into her bulging front pockets.

"And we *will* practice flexion."

With one foot, Anna Sorenson kicked open the hatch. She sat on the edge, her legs dangling in space.

"In the meantime, Homer," she said, "I got a crazy idea."

Right before she dropped to the rope, she smiled that crooked smile again and put it out there:

"Live."

Chapter *15*

After the hatch smacked shut, Homer and I stared at each other in silence. There was that grinding noise again and I peeked out to see a beat-up orange Volvo spinning out on the gravel driveway, spitting up dirt and dust and rocks on Mrs. Dinkins's little strip of flower garden.

"I thought she got here on a broom," I said quietly, resting my hands on the metal rail. "You okay?"

To my surprise, Homer smiled. "There's only one name for her," he said, his eyes wide.

I nodded in agreement. In the joint, she'd be classified a category J: crazy as a loon.

"J-Cat," we said together. I took his hand and stroked it.

"Sorry about letting her disrespect you," I said. "I didn't know how to start something up here. Maybe I can get your mom to call the agency and fire her."

"Don't say anything yet."

"Why? She's a buster, Homes."

Homer pressed his head against the pillow and rubbed at an itch.

"She's so crazy, Harry Sue, she just might be able to find my rock."

When he mentioned the rock, my heart sank like those two things had been tied together. The idea had snagged him and if it took hold, if he swallowed it the way a fish does a steel hook, he would be caught fast.

You can't hold out hope, dangle it in front of his nose like that, and then yank it away without serious consequences. I know this from the past.

"Don't look like that," he said. "I know I can't take back . . . what happened. I'm just curious is all. About what happens when things collide and how energy can flow . . ." Homer broke off there and pressed his lips together, willing himself not to cry.

It was the picture he had of himself at the bottom of Lake Michigan, Fish—that we both had—of the energy seeping out of him forever that made him so sad.

Should I believe what he said? Just curiosity? My instincts told me no. I still remember the days at the hospital after they stabilized him. And the tests they put him through.

"Concentrate, Christopher. Give it your best shot."

There was an army of them in pastel pantsuits and khakis. Everybody had a different way to unlock his motivation. They acted like he could *will* himself to move again.

There was the pretty one with the soft southern accent. "I think you can try a little harder, Mr. Dinkins. Just try? For me?"

And the bodybuilder who barked out commands to the sound track of *Fame*.

And the retired schoolteacher who made up a different acronym for Homer, depending on how he performed.

"I think we'll call you IAN today, which, of course, stands for 'inactivity achieves nothing,' Mr. Dinkins."

Homer was all over the map. He believed them. He cursed them. He wanted me to take 'em down. In the end, he just couldn't let them in anymore. He had to put up a big old wall around his broken self.

And finally, *finally* they went away.

Beau just let Homer do his time. He didn't try to make him do any special exercises. Just living through the day had got to be the biggest challenge Homer was up to facing.

That's why I wanted this J-Cat far away from

him. If I could, I would shoot her out of a cannon, send her back where she came from, melt her in a puddle of big ugly sundress.

"Harry Sue," Homer said quietly, drawing me back into the room with him. He was smiling. He looked up and to the right, asking me with his eyes to move a curl that had fallen over one of them, making him blink. I pinched it with two fingers and moved it back, then I let my whole hand smooth that shiny hair—just to make sure it stayed in place.

"Harry Sue, get out your notepad. I know how we're going to find your mom."

My hand left Homer's head to cover my mouth.

"For real?" I managed to whisper.

The whole time I was trying to find my mom, I believed with all my heart that my mom was trying to find me. I don't know why. How does Dorothy know that Aunt Em and Uncle Henry want her back again? How does she know they didn't find some other orphan to haul out to their new house on the prairie to handle the chores while she was gone?

I had evidence in my notepad. I put down every little thing, just hoping that all together it could make the case that Granny was doing her best to keep my Mary Bell from me.

Didn't Granny blame everything on Mary Bell? She blamed her for stealing Garnett. She blamed her for having the baby that made him drop out of community college. That's right, the same baby that got him locked up. She even blamed Mary Bell's genes for being so strong that, upon seeing me, most folks couldn't figure out what Garnett had to do with it. I looked that much like my mother. But most of all, she blamed Mary Bell for what happened to Garnett on the inside.

I believe that proves beyond a shadow of a doubt that Granny Clotkin was nut up. What happened to Garnett was my fault, Fish. His dying the way he did happened because of *me*, not my Mary Bell.

Walking back from Homer's house that day, I was full, not just of J-Cat, but of Homer's news, too. Another idea had caught in his head, one that would make me as happy as it would make him to walk again. And just because he knew nothing short of a miracle could make his dream come true didn't stop Homer Price from helping me realize mine.

And that, Fish, is the true meaning of a road dog.

Part 3
Lost

It was much harder to find their way back through the big fields of buttercups and yellow daisies than it was being carried. They knew, of course, they must go straight east, toward the rising sun; and they started off in the right way. But at noon, when the sun was over their heads, they did not know which was east and which was west, and that was the reason they were lost in the great fields.

—*The Wizard of Oz*

Chapter *16*

It was a sentence Beau had tossed off in passing that had snagged Homer's imagination, just like when I'd read that bit about trees absorbing energy. Something about the telephone answering system for the Wisconsin State Lottery.

What difference did it make to the price of tea in China, I wondered, that Wisconsin had an 800 number for buying lotto tickets? This was Michigan, not Wisconsin, and you could buy Quick Picks or the Daily Double at every gas station and drugstore in town.

But Homer was way ahead of me, seeing as the whole time I was rescuing Spooner from the pond and messing with the new teacher's art supplies and almost sending Violet Chump to her eternal re-ward, he was putting things together in his mind.

"First I had to make sure what Beau told me was right before I said anything. Then I had to call my-self. Well, I had the maternal unit call. Wisconsin is very progressive, Harry Sue. Even lumps like me, with a valid credit card, can participate in legalized gambling."

"Yeah, but why?" I wanted to know. "Your mom could just snag you a Daily Double at the gas station."

Homer smiled. He loved the dramatic pause.

"Well, not every lump has people to do his bid-ding. If your granny were laid up here, you think there'd be someone to wait on her? Maybe it's for people outside the state to call in their choices. *I don't know*, Harry Sue. Let's return to what matters here. What matters isn't that there is a telephone or-dering system. There is. What matters is that every telephone operator in the Wisconsin State Lottery is a conette."

Homer stopped one more time before he put it together for me. "There's a wealth of information to be gleaned here."

"You're playing me, Homes."

"No, this is for real, Harry Sue."

"They let those conettes have credit card num-bers?"

"There are safeguards in place. Besides, you

think they could have porch furniture from Land's End delivered to their cell block? What's a conette going to buy?"

"How about presents for her kids?"

"Well, the point is, they thought of all that," Homer said grumpily because, once again, we weren't going in the direction he wanted to. "They can't make any calls out."

I was about to argue they could memorize the numbers and pass them on to relatives. Let's face it. It's in my blood to know these things. But I didn't want to make Homer cross, so I let him go on with his story.

Well, almost. As he sat there, chewing his lip and waiting for me to jump on board, I thought of something else that troubled me.

"Why would you think she's in Wisconsin? She wasn't distributing across state lines, so it's not a federal crime. She's somewhere in Michigan, Homer, I just know it."

"You don't think conettes have friends? You don't think their hacks know hacks in Michigan? I bet they even go to the same conferences."

"But what are you driving at?"

Homer rolled his eyes. "My mom left it behind the Kleenex box. It's a good thing she tucked it away or that J-Cat might have stomped on it."

I fit my hand behind the Kleenex box and pulled out the Dinkins family cell phone.

"You want me to . . ."

"It's got to be you, Harry Sue. Number's taped to the back."

I turned the phone over. There it was, in Mrs. Dinkins's crabbed handwriting on a torn scrap of blue-lined notepaper. The 800 number for the Wisconsin State Lottery.

Of course it had to be me. I mean, Homer couldn't even pick up the phone to dial.

But what exactly was I doing?

I looked at Homer's excited face and realized that if I didn't get excited with him, I was gonna burn the spot. And I realized this was as much about Homer as it was about me. He was trying to have my back the only way left to him, by bringing me my Mary Bell. When I looked at it that way, I thought what was so wrong with asking for a little information?

I pressed the numbers in and waited. First thing I heard was music. Happy orchestra music. Soaring trombones. Big drums. It was music for winners, I realized. Music to get you in the mood.

"Welcome to the Wisconsin State Lottery," a nice voice said. "Please pay attention, as the following menu selections have changed. For English, press one. *Para español, dos.*"

Homer's eyebrows were raised. He wanted the play-by-play.

"I chose English."

The nice voice came back on. "To order the Daily Dole, press one. To order the Instant Millionaire, press two. To check the winning numbers for a previous date, press three. . . ." I listened to the whole menu, but it wasn't until after "To repeat the selection process, press eight" that I heard the one I wanted.

"To speak to a customer service representative, press nine."

A tight band pressed around my chest. There was a clicking noise and I heard the soothing lady come back on. She said, "Connecting to an operator. Your call may be monitored to ensure quality service."

"They're connecting me," I told Homer.

"Jeez, it takes long enough." He'd been straining in his bed for so long he had to relax back onto his pillows.

I started to ask him just what I was supposed to say, expecting more music or the nice lady or just waiting. But I heard another voice, a real voice I had to strain to understand because she spoke with a heavy accent.

"Welcome to the Wisconsin State Lottery," she said. "My name is Consuela. How may I help you?"

"Uh . . ." I looked at Homer helplessly. Was I really supposed to spill my guts?

"Yes?" the voice with the name Consuela said.

"Consuela, are you . . . do you . . . ?"

"Are you having some trouble with the system?" Consuela prompted.

It took me a second to figure out what she said because it sounded like "see-stem."

"It's just . . ." I glanced helplessly at Homer, who was mouthing the word "mom."

"I'm looking for my mom," I said in a rush. "She's a conette."

There was a long pause. *"Dios mio,"* Consuela said. Then the clicking noise. Then the nice lady. "If you feel you have reached this number in error . . ."

I pressed the "end" button on the phone.

"What? What?" Homer asked, all excited. He was using his shoulder to get a little leverage, bouncing his head back and forth. It was how he underlined his words. How he said, *I really want this!*

"She hung up on me," I said.

Homer made me repeat the conversation word for word, including all the selection options.

"Dios mio," he said slowly. "That means 'my God.'"

He smiled and gave me his "aha" look. "Consuela's going to help us," he said.

"What makes you think that?"

"She said, 'My God.' It's hardly like saying, 'Get lost, kid.'"

"But she hung up on me."

"So?"

"I see that as a sign of rejection."

Homer sighed. "Harry Sue, you've got to have patience."

He nestled back into his pillows, smiling. "We'll call her again tomorrow."

Chapter *17*

I didn't get home in time to see the kids off. Sink and Dip had just finished painting their nails and were eating the leftover snacks, pushing stick pretzels to the edge of the counter with their palms and pinching them so as not to disturb the drying polish.

Hunger squeezed my stomach as I opened the fridge, looking for something decent to eat. I was inspecting a piece of American cheese for fuzz when Granny burst through the door, looking like she wanted to bust some heads.

"I tell ya, that nigra's movin' in!" she shouted at no one in particular.

Sink looked at Dip and rolled her eyes.

"Now, Gran," she said. "Maybe he's the gardener."

To Dip, she said, "Gran seen him through her binoculars this morning cutting the grass down the block."

"That house that's been vacant?" Dip asked. "But Granny, you said you didn't care who lived there long as somebody started taking care of the place."

"I draw the line at nigras!" Granny whirled around to face Sink, her eyes wild.

"He was carrying a chair. Into the house!" she screamed, like that was a federal crime. "What kind of lousy gardener carries chairs?"

Dip was rubbing at her eye and forgot the nail polish, smearing it on her cheek.

"Gran!" she complained.

But old Granny was far away, being consumed by her discovery. She slammed the carpetbag she called a purse onto the counter and fished out her cell phone.

"Put on Eunice Baker," she shouted into the phone. "Eunice, you old windbag. I told you that nigra was moving in this morning. Now what's gonna happen to these house prices?"

Granny paused and we heard the whine that was Eunice's voice, trying to calm her down. "What difference does it make if he's African? Where I come from, black is black!"

She listened a minute longer before throwing the phone back into her purse in disgust.

Granny was old-school, born in Detroit to a family who settled there long before black people moved up north in search of work in what we learned in school was the Great Migration. Sometimes she even called it Old Detroit, and we all knew what she meant. She meant white Detroit. If we'd been on speaking terms, I might have mentioned that the Indians were here even before Detroit came along.

Granny's hate was so bad it was illegal, Fish. If black people showed up at our door looking for day care, Granny told them she was just full that morning. Got her reported once when the very same lady called that afternoon and Granny said she had three openings.

Funny how her hate sometimes worked in my favor. Because of Granny's preferences, I knew a whole mess of crumb snatchers were safe from her wicked ways. Me, I didn't have a preference, but Beau says in the joint, you hang with your own kind. Black with black, white with white, Asian with Asian, Latino with Latino.

I spent considerable time figuring that out. Seems to me, we all bleed red. But then again, I don't make the rules. I'll just have to live by them.

"His name is Mr. Olatanju," I told Sink and Dip, surprising myself by pronouncing it perfectly.

Now that I had everyone's attention, I took my time giving up the information. I'd moved along to a piece of bread and started pinching off the green spots.

"He's my new art teacher," I added.

Granny looked pretty cheesed off to have her information confirmed. Far as I remember, she only had three looks: "mad as hell," "scheming," and "lovable-but-worn-out day-care provider." She started using her purse to do a bicep curl. Whenever she was really worked up, Granny started pumping stuff. I've seen her do a grab and lift with a seventy-pound crumb snatcher who accidentally pulled a few flowers while weeding the front garden. She had worked up quite a sweat by the time the doorbell rang.

Granny disappeared into the hall. First we heard the door swing open, then the sound of something breaking into pieces on the cement front stoop.

Then Granny's voice: "Don't try to give me any of that poison African crap," she screamed. "You! You go back where you came from. We don't mix with nigras and you're blacker than most. Now go on off my porch. Don't want no nigras round here."

I had crept into the hall to get another look at my teacher as he towered over Granny. His head was down, looking at his hands.

"I was told that you have been asking about me." He spoke slowly. "Knowing how you feel, it must be a relief to discover up close that I am not black."

"What's that supposed to mean?" Granny spit out. She was on her guard.

"For myself, I was much relieved . . . ," he continued, looking now into the distance, ignoring her question. It wasn't hard to trump Granny in the thought department, especially when she was mad. I inched closer, still staying out of sight.

"You see, I have a habit of disliking cranky women, white women who throw down my cooking without a taste. Yes, it's true. I have a real prejudice against bitter, dried-up shrews. But seeing up close that you are not white gives me much relief as well."

There was a grittiness in his voice like the teeth in the back of his mouth were touching when he spoke. I realized that if I came forward at that moment, he would hate me now, as he hated Granny, would think of us as road dogs and mark me as his enemy.

And today wouldn't be such an awful waste.

So why was it so hard to pull myself forward and into the light and to pretend that Granny was in my crew? I held back. But then I told myself that this African was slow to hate, and desperate times call for desperate measures, which is something I read in a book somewhere and, unfortunately, had a lot of cause to remember.

So I did it.

"Harry Sue?" he said, sounding all confused.

I sure did like the way he said my name. And then he surprised me with a smile, a big one, like he was seeing an old friend, and he held out his hand to me, but Granny slapped it away.

"Nobody touches her," Granny said. "And I'm as white as they come, you dirty nigra. Don't you dare say I ain't. I'm an American!"

He kept looking at me and smiling, as if her words were having no effect on him whatsoever.

Just before she slammed the door, he said quietly: "This explains much, my friend."

And to Granny, through the door: "You may keep the dish. It is a present from Sudan."

Sink and Dip had crept up behind us. Granny ordered Sink to get the broom.

When Sink came back with it, Granny said, "Get somebody out there to pick up that crap."

Sink turned to me and started to repeat Granny's words. Normally, I'd just let the broom and dustpan clatter to the floor, but not today. I was curious.

I went outside. I picked at the big pieces of pottery. They were burnt orange, like the color of the sun just before it slides off the earth in the summer. And there was such a smell there, like dirt after a rain. Only sweeter. It made my stomach put up quite a fuss. So I pinched a chunk of meat that lay in one of the bigger pieces of the dish and put it in my mouth. It melted on my tongue, sweet and hot and tender. I took another piece of something green: a pepper, I think, and it tasted the same, only with a bit of crunch. I reached into my shirt pocket and pulled out the slice of bread I'd been working on when Mr. Olatanju arrived at the door. I dipped it in some of the gravy, careful not to eat anything that had touched the ground. It made even Granny's stale white bread taste like a holiday.

I glanced up to see her peering down at me through the little window in the front door. I heard her slide in the dead bolt, locking me out.

I just gave Granny a big smile and took another bite.

Chapter *18*

"Now, Harry Sue, honey, you're not going to break the law or hurt any innocent children with this, are you?" Mrs. Dinkins asked as she handed me a big creased grocery bag folded down and held together with a chip clip.

We were standing in her kitchen and, with the light streaming in, I noticed how faded it had all become. Her clothes, the curtains, even the countertops and the plates looked like they'd been there in just that position for more years than I'd been on this earth.

She was wearing the loose shirt and baggy khaki pants I'd seen on her a hundred times before. It made me think that she probably hadn't gone shopping for anything new to wear since the day the phone call came in from the Ottawa County Sheriff's Department.

"Mrs. Dinkins," I said, forcing myself to breathe in. "The only people I hurt are the ones who deserve it. It's called the school of hard knocks. There are just some people who need to learn that Harry Sue doesn't take it on the chin."

But Homer's mom wasn't listening. She was kneading her shoulder and looking out the window in the direction of the tree house.

"She's up there again," she said, worry stirring up the words. "That therapy woman. She's got ideas, Harry Sue. Things she wants to try on Christopher. But I don't know about all that. Gettin' his hopes up. Comin' down is so hard."

But I wasn't really listening to her, either. I was wondering if you could suffocate on dust. There was so much dust here, hanging heavy in the air. The sun pointed to it. I knew if I grabbed the curtains, they would cough dust. The whole house was covered in an avalanche of dust. . . .

I needed air, so I held up the bag and said, "Thanks for this, and don't worry, Mrs. Dinkins," knowing full well that was like telling a shark not to swim. Worry was how she got from four-thirty to five-fifteen and from five-fifteen to six-thirty.

But right now I couldn't attend to Mrs. Dinkins. I needed to see Homer and to tell him about what had happened with Granny and the art teacher. I wanted to tell him how you could win a fight with Granny without throwing a punch, how Mr. Olatanju had scored a KO by telling Granny she wasn't white, which was pretty much the same as if he'd caught her on the chin.

Yes, I knew J-Cat was there. Hadn't I seen the Volvo, two tires over the curb? I put the bag in my teeth, unhooked the rope, and started to climb, hoping she was nearly through turning Homer and airing his butt. But as I got near to the hatch, I heard a sound like my worst nightmare exploding in my ears. It was coming from Homer, coming from his throat. He was coughing on something and he couldn't even turn himself over.

As soon as I hauled myself into the tree house, I bit down on the chip clip out of shock, spilling Mrs. Dinkins's bra, the batteries, the tennis balls, and the wire all over the floor. That's because, before I even got a glimpse of Homer, I saw J-Cat, spread-eagled on the other side of the picture window. Her ugly sundress flapped around her bony knees, which were making two red circles on the glass. She was doing something that little kids do, smushing her face into the glass, making her lips look like helpless worms, her nose like a prizefighter's.

And Homer . . . Homer was laughing.

I lay on the floor, panting, relief and anger competing inside me.

"Harry Sue? You okay?" Homer was craning his neck to see me.

I pulled myself up and stood next to his head. "I just thought . . . the noise . . ."

I stopped and looked up at J-Cat, who'd made both hands into circles and was looking through them at me like she was peering through a pair of binoculars.

How could I tell Homer I didn't recognize the sound of his laughter?

Chapter 19

"Harry Sue's got boobs! Would ya look at those?"

My new figure was causing quite a stir as we lined up for class the next morning.

"Yeah, right," Nick Nederman said. "That's a boob job. You can't grow those things overnight."

Waterhead. Like he knew what he was talking about.

Ms. Lanier looked me over. She knew there was more to my hooters than the hard round bumps that met her eye. But the morning bell rang and there was milk money to collect and attendance to take and a whole list of other boring teacher-type things to attend to.

I just smiled and waited for the thoughts to

connect in Jolly Roger's small brain that, come recess time, he should grab hold of my bra strap and give it a good yank.

I'll tell you one thing, with all the itching and the adjusting, I have no idea whatsoever why girls make such a fuss over growing these things.

Meanwhile, Violet was mooning over me like I was her new boyfriend.

"Ma says we're gonna have you over for dinner, Harry Sue, for a thank-you." She leaned in close to me and whispered, "You like chicken-fried steak? What you got stuffed in there, anyway? I put a little Kleenex in mine sometimes, but that's not really cheating. Rosejane says they got padded ones with little foam things called 'cookies' down at Sears in the Marshfield Mall, but Ma says I might as well wait until the real ones show up, else why do people always want to invite trouble?"

My, she rattled on, bumpin' her gums about every imaginable thing. I realized then I didn't have to worry so much about punishing myself for saving her. Having to listen to Violet go on about brassieres and foam cookies might just be worse than lockdown.

We were inside by now, sitting at our desks. Ms. Lanier was up front working out a math problem. As if the numbers weren't confusing enough, now she was adding letters to the mix.

"If x equals six," she said.

My question was this: If x equals six, why don't people just say so and be done with it? And while we're at it, what worldly purpose does a girl like Violet Chump serve? She couldn't KO a baby bunny, nor did she have the sense of a chicken-fried steak. I mean, the Scarecrow in *The Wizard of Oz* had more brains than her with just straw stuffed in a burlap sack.

I sighed, thinking about the long road ahead of me. I can tell you right now, it wasn't made of yellow brick. Not since I got me another misfit for my crew, somebody I'd have to protect from Jolly Roger, somebody whose tears I'd be mopping up with the worn-out hem of my skirt.

That's the kind of reward I get when I stick my neck out.

Still and all, I thought, trying to look at the bright side, I was partial to edible food of any kind and chicken-fried steak, just the idea of it, was making my mouth water. I never did figure how Dorothy got to be so plump and rosy-cheeked. If you read that book, you'll see for yourself all she ever eats until she gets to Oz is nuts and bread and a piece of fruit now and then. I rubbed at the tennis balls banded against my chest to relieve the terrible itch and settled in until recess.

In the joint, you get respect for being plain. Harry Sue does not play mind games. She lets you know right up front when it's on. That way, you can decide whether to put it down and back away or enter in of your own free will. I always gave the boys a taste of what they had coming. That way, if they decided to bite, it was their own fool business.

At recess, those boys circled around me like a pack of hungry wolves.

"Nice potatoes, Harry Sue. I guess you really are a girl."

"And a fine girl like me deserves to be treated with a little respect," I said, rearranging my boobies. "So don't be touching any parts of me or you're in for the shock of your life."

"Not much of a shock to discover them things aren't real," Nick said. Thought he was a regular PhD, Nick did. I knew a cell warrior when I saw one. Got lots to say in a crowd, but get him alone with a shank at his throat and he'll PC up in a hurry.

"I'm talking a real shock here. Watts, amps, sizzle."

I don't think I could have made it much plainer.

But the problem with these juveniles is they have no impulse control. They weren't even hearing me. Jolly Roger glanced around at his road dogs with a look that said, *Ready?*

They looked back. *Oh, yeah,* and started to close in.

"All right, gentlemen," I said, "but don't say you weren't warned." And I took off running so they'd get a clear shot at my back because, of course, that's where the trigger was.

Chapter 20

"There's only one person in Trench Vista history who could dream up a mechanism like this," Mr. Hernandez said, peeling back the outer covering of a tennis ball and extracting a taped bundle of industrial, size-C batteries. "And that's Christopher Dinkins.

"Christopher Dinkins," he repeated, putting his hands behind his head and leaning back in his chair. "Now, there was a boy with promise. Do you remember his science project, Harry Sue, on the trajectory of spitballs? I tell you, that modest little display taught our students more about physics than I could accomplish in a weeklong unit at the middle school.

"What promise . . ." He sighed and shook his head. "How's he doing?"

"Fine," I mumbled, careful not to show Mr. Hernandez any respect *and* to let him know I did not want to get into it about Homer.

"I really should go visit."

He had turned in his seat and was looking out the window now, talking more to himself than to me. "I'm sure time weighs heavy after an accident like that. His mother is homeschooling him, I hear."

I wanted to tell him not to bother about the visit, that he'd never make it up the rope in his condition, and furthermore, what would he say once he got there? That Homer had promise?

That was all I needed.

Mr. Hernandez rubbed at his eyes under his glasses and turned back to face me.

"But let us return to you, Miss Clotkin." He lifted up Mrs. Dinkins's frayed old brassiere. "There is nothing in the Trench Vista code of conduct that covers electrocuting one's peers via the metal stays of a device solely intended for the purpose of keeping body parts from shifting during transit."

To my extensive relief, he dropped the bra and thumbed through the rule book again, just in case.

"In point of fact," he continued, "we don't cover electrocuting at all." He looked up at me and sighed again. "Could it be that the architects of this document underestimated the intelligence of our students? Or could it be, Harry Sue, that the mastermind of this plan has more time on his hands than he knows what to do with?"

Without meaning to, I gave Mr. Hernandez a look.

This look was not in the current edition of the Harry Sue catalog of looks. But over the next couple weeks, I decided it had to be in the next one. I used it that much. It was the look the Wizard gave Dorothy when she called him a phony.

Bingo, said the look. *You got that right.*

Mr. Hernandez seemed satisfied.

"Well, in any case, Mr. Olatanju will have you this afternoon for detention regarding the little matter of ruining eighteen perfectly good squeeze bottles of finger paint. That will give me time to meditate upon the matter of the highly charged brassiere."

He put his two hands, with ten perfectly manicured fingernails, on the top of his desk and pushed away, rolling back in his chair.

"Oh, and will anyone be needing this?" he asked as he stood up, the brassiere dangling from one crooked finger.

"Yeah," I mumbled, reaching out my hand, my gaze on the floor.

I didn't have my backpack with me, so I had to crush the bra as small as possible in my fist. I wasn't halfway to Mr. Olatanju's office when my hand started to sweat. It was all I could do to hold on to the thing, knowing where it had been and where it would return.

There wasn't much to live on over at Homer's house, but Jeez, couldn't she at least get something new to put there? Not so worn and frayed you had to feel sorry for her boobs on top of everything else?

When I came to the door of the art room, I smelled that smell again, like a tickle in my nose, like outside air after lockdown in Granny's closet, smelling her sour smell for refusing to eat her rotten cooking. Or like rolling down the window after being pinched between Sink and Dip in the car, their cheap foo foo mixing with Granny's cigar smoke while the Lawrence Welk Orchestra blasted from the speakers.

"Harry Sue, you are most welcome." He reached out again with his big hand but stopped himself halfway. Dropping his arm, Mr. Olatanju made a little bow.

"In Sudan, where I come from, it is a custom to eat before intention," he said.

"Detention," I corrected him, stepping back so that my shoulder blades touched the wall.

"Yes, of course." He nodded seriously. "But first, we welcome our guests with a little drink of fruit juice to refresh them after their long journey."

I was about to say I only just came down the hall from Mr. Hernandez, but my nose got me distracted. Mr. Olatanju had cleared off one of the art tables and covered it with fresh butcher paper. At the center of the table was a vase filled with tissue-paper flowers. Next to that sat a fat orange jug with steam curling out of the spout. There was also a big pitcher and a bowl that looked like they were made out of hammered pennies. Behind him, on his desk, sat two mud-colored dishes with lids decorated in swirls of yellow with black-and-white dots, and two plates with what looked like big spongy pancakes on them.

I took the little glass he held out to me. I thought it was lemonade, but it tasted so sour.

"Just a little grapefruit juice," he said. "Not too sweet to spoil the appetite."

The smells that curled around me were so strong they made promises. I tried to remember what I'd eaten that day, a handful of dried cereal at breakfast and one chicken strip for lunch since I had to spend most of my time in the bathroom making sure the wires hadn't come loose.

Mr. Olatanju took up the pitcher and said, "Now, let us rinse off the dust of the road before we eat."

I was supposed to do something, but I didn't know what. I knew I couldn't keep one hand behind my back the whole time, so I came to the table and sat down, dropping Mrs. Dinkins's bra under my seat.

"Yes, just put your hands over the bowl."

I stuck my hands over the penny bowl and Mr. Olatanju poured water over them. The water was so cold it made my fingers ache, but I felt cleaner, too, like there was a cold river between what had happened in Mr. Hernandez's office and what was happening now. He handed me a towel and I rubbed my hands dry.

"I'm afraid our time is too short to have a proper meal," he said, going over to his desk and pulling two tiny cups from his drawer. He set them in front of me and poured from the steaming pot.

"Today, we'll drink our chai with the meal. Normally, in Sudan, we drink nothing at the meal, but things cannot stay the same always, can they, Harry Sue?"

Bingo. You got that right.

As he set the dishes down, I wondered if anyone had set a table for me since Mary Bell got sentenced. I didn't think so.

Mr. Olatanju nodded seriously and took his seat, shaking out his napkin with a snap. I realized I was sitting on mine, so I pulled it out from underneath me and smoothed it over my lap.

As he took the cover off one of the dishes, the powerful smell took me far away to someplace exotic where big jungle birds with shiny beaks and wings that looked like rays of the sun were taking flight.

I knew then I was so hungry I would never

make it back to Granny's under my own power, or up Homer's rope, for that matter.

Mr. Olatanju was all business. "This is *kisra*," he said, pointing to the soft round bread on the plate. "We tear a small piece and use it to pinch the food in the pot, like so."

He was so careful with his big fingers. When I tried to pinch the meat, my bread dropped into the bowl.

"No problem," he said, smiling as he fished it out with a fork and put it on my plate. "The practice breads are just as tasty."

Like the dish I'd tasted two days before, there was nothing hard to chew here. The bread, the sauce, the meat melted away to nothing.

Suddenly, my throat was so dry, it started to close. It was a familiar feeling, the one that came just before crying.

Somehow, Mr. Olatanju understood what was happening. He put his big warm hand on my wrist.

"Yes, Harry Sue," he said. "It is the same with me. You see, Mr. Hernandez gave me your file."

I thought this was my cue to tell the story, and for one second I wanted him to make me tell it so the smells that whirled around me like a spell would turn sour and give off the odor of rain-rotted leaves and make me lose my appetite.

But instead, Mr. Olatanju pinched a piece of

meat with a small scrap of bread and handed it to me.

"When we eat together like this, Harry Sue, we are reminded of the homes we no longer have. That is why the food tastes so . . . how do you say it . . . distinctive. This smell"— he waved his arm to take it all in: the spicy tea, the sour juice, the delicious meat—"is my mother. Sometimes, I cry when I make it."

There went the look again.

Bingo. You got that right.

A small part of me started giving myself the lecture that began with, "Do your own time, Harry Sue."

I wrestled it down and pointed to the other dish, the one that was still covered.

"Can I try what's in there?"

Chapter 21

While we ate, it began to rain. I didn't notice it in Mr. Olatanju's art room, where it seemed like my stomach was filling with sunshine, but on the way home the sky was as close as the drop ceiling in Granny's basement, and rain pelted my face and shoulders. On days like this, the crumb snatchers had to spend the whole day in the basement, in the small room next to the boiler that Granny called the playroom. By now, though, they should be at their post in the living room, waiting for me to get home.

Though I expected her to be at bingo, Granny's ancient Chevrolet Impala was parked in its place by the door, a red plastic whiffle bat pinned under one wheel.

I scanned the windows for my crew, but the

room was empty, so I started to run, snagging my backpack on Licensed and Loving and yanking so hard to get it free I made the sign groan in protest.

Sink and Dip were clustered in a corner of the kitchen, eating Cheese Nips and pretending to read a soap rag, but the minute I came in, they dropped the magazine.

"Where's Moonie Pie?"

"Still in the tub," Sink said. "We figured it'd be safer."

I stood still and sniffed the air, trying to catch the scent of tears. Something was wrong, very wrong, but even so, I would check on Moonie Pie quick before heading down to the basement and doing the count.

"What's on?" I asked them with a look that said, *Give it up, fools. Now!*

"Granny says the bingo money's gone out of her purse." Sink chewed hard on a hangnail.

"She's just mad 'cause she left the lights on in her Impala last night and the battery's dead." Dip rolled her eyes. "Wolf Man'd never take her money."

On the inside, you will have a decision to make, Fish. You will meet the hardest hacks and the lousiest cons. And there will come a time when you have to make up your mind about joining them. Some cons and some hacks hit the joint yoked up and talking tough, but Sink and Dip were taking the slow route. They could stay up in the kitchen, their hands wrist-deep in Cheese Nips, even though they knew Wolf Man didn't do anything wrong. And he was just a little kid. You do that enough times and you'll turn lousy, too, Fish.

I needed just a minute to get hold of myself, to pry open the fist that had grabbed my happy stomach. For an hour that day I had been on the outs, smelling things and tasting things no conette has the right to enjoy. It was time to get back to the joint.

I made the stairs in about three steps to find Moonie Pie had pulled himself up and was busy gnawing the side of the tub with that one tooth he was so fond of. He left off chewing to gaze up at me, his face filled with the kind of happiness that says, *All my dreams have come true.*

I put my hands under his armpits and pulled his plump little body toward me. His bottom was cold and wet and his feet were bare again, but he still had that sleepy baby smell in his hair. He patted my hands and face and crooned to me in his baby language. Soon he would be old enough to hoist himself out of the tub, and I felt a brief flutter of panic at the thought of him teetering at the top of the stairs while Sink and Dip, their hair covered in shower caps, gave themselves highlights.

"I'll be right back," I said. "Promise."

As I put him down, he looked up at me and bit

his little lip. His eyes filled with tears, but he didn't cry. Before I left Moonie Pie behind, I snuggled those perfect feet back into his booties and thought to myself, *Now there's a kid knows how to do his own time.* We both flinched as we heard a crash coming from the basement.

Homer says you can feel a tornado. The pressure of the air changes and your skin just knows. I imagine Dorothy must have known when she went after Toto that the twister was about to hit.

Since there was no screaming, I figured Granny was working out some mental terrorism. Wolf Man was like me, couldn't stand to see others hurt. So chances were, she was going after Carly Mae and letting him watch.

Think. Think!

I tore down the steps and pulled the straightened paper clip from beneath the sofa in the living room, the one I used to pick the lock on Granny's curio cabinet. There was China Country laid out in front of me. *Were they happy to be sprung?* I wondered as I reached in and grabbed a handful. Most went straight to my backpack and under the couch, but I held on to that stupid little Dutch girl leaning forward for a kiss.

She was about to get hers.

I dropped her into my shirt pocket and headed for the basement. Just a little watery grayness filtered through the windows. When my eyes adjusted, I found the crumb snatchers pushed into one corner of the cramped playroom.

The sound I'd heard was Granny beating the liver and lights out of Carly Mae's stuffed bear, Oswald. It lay helpless on the colored-plastic play table while she brought a broom handle down on it again and again. Wolf Man was trying to protect Carly Mae from witnessing the beating. She was pressed behind him, one fist in her mouth, tears streaming down her face, snot running out of her nose.

Granny might just as well have been tuning up Carly Mae.

"You. Still. Don't. Know. Nothing?" Granny asked, dropping all the acts and becoming just exactly what she was. Hadn't Mr. Olatanju said it—a bitter, dried-up shrew?

Wolf Man shook his head, the corners of his mouth low. He didn't know how to lie.

Granny brought the broomstick down one more time. A plastic eye flew off Oswald and Carly Mae choked back a sob. Wolf Man looked like he might die right there, standing up.

Sit up, Fish! This is important. A conette needs to keep her cool. I'm telling you true because this time it was harder for me than ever before. This time I wanted to jump. I wanted to leap off the cliff I was always on with Granny. Just one step and my life of violent crime could begin.

But I didn't do it. Because out of the corner of my eye, I saw Hammer Head standing off to the side with a real, honest-to-goodness hammer in his hand, looking like he was about to commit a capital offense that might net him fifty years and change.

Time for the show.

"Good afternoon, children," I said in my mock-Granny-mock-welcome-to-the-parents voice.

Granny straightened and turned toward me, cocking the broom like a baseball bat. There were those red-rimmed eyes again, glowing like a light-up witch at Halloween.

"Granny's been so busy giving you quality care she forgot the art project for today. We're gonna make a sand painting," I continued, pulling the little Dutch girl out of my pocket. "But we need supplies. We need . . . sand."

I held up the innocent china girl with just one thing on her mind, a little smooch. As I spoke, I walked slowly toward Hammer Head. "So I figure we crush this porcelain baby up real good . . . with this!" I grabbed the hammer with my free hand and held it up. Hammer Head held on, too. "And voilà! Colored sand."

I took my eyes off Granny for one second to whisper, "I see you givin' her the green light, but let's wait until there are no witnesses, okay?"

Hammer Head gave me a smirk and released

his grip. A big sigh escaped me. One less juvenile would be crowding the county courthouse today.

But taking my eyes off Granny had been a mistake. Just as I was near the edge with her, Granny was toeing the same line.

I looked up to see her advancing toward me, swinging her broomstick wildly.

"To scratch with my promise," she said through her clenched teeth, red blotches firing up her cheeks.

"Tell her to give that back. *Now!*"

"You talking to me?" I grabbed Hammer Head by the hand and leapt onto the couch, bouncing from foot to foot to release the pent-up energy. I had a sudden image of J-Cat swinging from the rafters in Homer's tree house and it made me laugh out loud and bounce even higher.

"Do you know why we're going to hit this smoochy girl with a hammer?" I asked the crew. "Because she took Granny's bingo money and she's not sorry."

It was almost funny watching Granny's face work it out. She wanted me, all right. She wanted me *so bad.* The only thing standing in her way was the pretty little piece of china I held in my hand.

She cared more about this dead thing than the real live baby upstairs in the bathtub. Or the sniffling crumb snatchers frozen in place on the basement floor. I could maybe even hold Sink and Dip hostage with a gun, and it wouldn't matter so much as long as I didn't start shooting in the vicinity of her curio cabinet.

And then a thought struck me out of the blue so hard I staggered around on the couch a minute.

If I got the heart I kept asking for, the one made out of riveted steel, the one that would help me survive the joint . . .

I would be just like Granny.

She was what you turned into when you had a heart that didn't feel.

The Wizard was wrong. Beau was wrong. The Tin Man was right.

"Once I had brains and a heart also," he said. "Having tried them both, I should much rather have a heart."

"Give it here," she spat out, jabbing her broomstick at me.

I glanced over at the mostly terrified crumb snatchers.

I wouldn't be able to see their terror.

I wouldn't know when Homer was getting close to the hole.

My brain would magnify a little sliver of interest so that it consumed me. How could I win more at bingo and fill my cupboards with sparkly crap? How many winners over ten thousand in the Daily Double?

And then, once I made it to the joint, it would be

how to score personals off the fish and get a job in the prison canteen instead of washing blues.

Dios mio, I thought, and I almost dropped the smoochy girl.

I don't want that.

I bounced around that couch, dodging Granny's broomstick and probably looking to all the world as if I'd gone nut up. But only I knew what was happening inside me. Things were breaking apart, Fish, they were shifting around. Something moved into my throat and tried to push its way out, but I swallowed it down. No way would I ever show it to Granny.

Even though I felt like crying, I felt good, too. Relieved. Like all I'd been getting all those years were down letters, and now I might just score parole. And it was all because I realized that maybe I wouldn't have to become a hard-core criminal to find my way home. Maybe there was another way for Mary Bell to come to me. I couldn't see it just yet, but neither could Dorothy and her crew when they were in the forest of fighting trees, and that didn't stop them from going forward.

I shook my head and eyeballed Granny. Seemed to me like she was the big obstacle here. But then, I'd never had any bargaining power before. Maybe we could deal.

I dropped smoochy girl back in my pocket and grabbed the end of Granny's broomstick.

"Granny, dear," I said, speaking slow and looking her in the eye. "I'd be happy to exchange this little china girl for any letters you might be holding on to. Letters to do with me."

There, I'd said it.

Granny was too far gone down the path of beating me senseless and hiding my body under the floorboards to mask the look on her face.

It was the look that said, *Bingo!*

Chapter 22

That look was all I needed. Far as I was concerned, I could throw my notepad away.

"How do you know about that letter?" Granny asked, still clenching the bat.

"Doesn't matter how I know. They're mine."

"Is not!"

Suddenly, all eyes turned toward the ceiling as we heard the daily parade of tires on gravel. Granny swore under her breath and threw down the broom.

I looked around at the terrified faces of the crumb snatchers, knowing I had to bring them back to some safe place.

"Children!" I said in my falsy voice. "Where does the time go? We've been so busy viciously assaulting this stuffed bear that we couldn't start our art project."

I hopped off the couch and swooped up the button eye. I knew I should give Oswald back to Carly Mae just the way he was. What a seed for the garden of doubt I was planting about Granny's abilities. Yes, Granny would have some fancy explaining to do to Wanda.

But as I looked at Carly Mae's mouth full of fist and her wet blotchy cheeks, I just couldn't bring myself to hand over the bear.

"Oswald needs to go to the hospital tonight," I told her. "But he's coming back tomorrow. And he'll be all better. I promise."

I nodded to Wolf Man. "Clean her up, okay?" He put his arm protectively around Carly Mae and headed for the stairs.

I stood back and looked at the others. With the exception of Hammer Head, who had taken back the hammer and was smacking it against his palm, they still looked like they were playing a game of freeze tag.

"Well, c'mon," I said. "Pull yourselves together. It's show time!"

I pointed upstairs to China Country. "Be sure to take inventory, dear Granny," I said, "because this little peasant girl isn't the only one you're missing. I'll give you one day. Tomorrow. After Homer's, at the latest. I want those letters."

• • •

As soon as I was out of sight of Granny's kitchen window, I held up, right there at the edge of Mrs. Mead's garden. Granny does not encourage fraternizing with the neighbors, so I didn't spend much time talking with Mrs. Mead, but still I thought of her as my friend. She could make anything spring out of the hard clay soil we lived on. If she could coax life out of a brick, then odds were my smoochy girl would be safe on her property for just a day or two.

The spot where she rested her garbage can each week made a perfect nest of dried grass. Seeing as we had four more days to garbage day, I placed the figurine there as carefully as a mother bird places her egg. She was ransom for my own mother, after all, and I didn't want to take a chance on breaking her.

I stood there for a minute, looking down at the little porcelain doll. She was nothing. She didn't feel. She didn't care if I cracked her with a rock. The pieces would still be waiting for a kiss. How Granny could trade her for the kisses of a real child, I didn't know.

Still, the meanings of things can change. I cared a lot more for that piece of china now than I had yesterday. I pulled the roll of toilet paper I'd snagged from the bathroom out of my pack and wrapped her good and tight in it.

Stepping back, I pressed my hands against my hot face. My shoulder throbbed like it always did after a standoff with Granny. When I faced her, I forgot everything: my mind, my body, my arms, my legs. Now I didn't know what was happening. I felt dizzy.

On the one hand, there was this terrible pain shooting through my shoulder and across my back. On the other, there was incredible joy.

There were letters! She really was trying to write me!

I didn't have to end up like Granny. I could be like other kids. Maybe Mary Bell was coming back soon. Maybe she would get a job in another state and take me away from this place.

When Mary Bell showed up, she was going to fix all the things that were broken.

My feet started to find their way to Homer's house.

Of course, I couldn't leave Homer and the rest of my crew behind when I shook the spot. I'd have to take them with me. And we'd live in a big old house with a front porch, maybe near a park with a decent place to play for the little road dogs. And I'd even let old Violet hang around, as long as she was on the low and brought plenty of that chicken-fried steak.

Grabbing my shoulder, I squeezed, and little icicles of pain shot down my neck. I squeezed again. You probably won't understand this, Fish, but at that moment, it felt so good just to feel.

Chapter 23

I tried not to let the sight of J-Cat's bruised and beat-up Volvo ruin the delicious pain I was feeling. I had information for Homer and I was gonna give it up. But not in front of her.

As I pulled myself up, the whole tree house shook with the sound of something very heavy rolling on the floor.

"Can't see it now, can you, Homer, my boy?" I heard her scratched voice even before I pushed open the hatch.

"Another customer!" she cried as I pulled myself up. "Come in, come in, and take a seat up front. You see, Homer, it's like those free vacations in Mexico. You can have a lovely conversation about old times with your slab of rock here, *but* first you have to listen to the sales pitch."

I stood up and saw that Homer was crying. The way his lips were pressed together and his breathing was heavy, I knew these weren't normal tears.

These tears burned his cheeks with frustration. They were furious tears. Homer wanted to kill her.

Suddenly, all the feelings that raged inside me earlier threatened to break free. I took Homer's cold hand and held on for dear life.

"All right, then," she said, digging through her enormous pockets.

It was then I noticed the rock. A rock that must have weighed nearly what she did. I couldn't imagine how she'd hauled it up here.

It was still wet, this rock. I stared at the dark stain the water made as it seeped into the plywood floor.

"This is you," J-Cat said, unfolding a picture she must have drawn herself of a stick figure, its little legs and arms bent into the shape of a person running.

She turned the paper over. "This is you with a C4 spinal injury."

The new figure was sprawled on its back. Its little eyes were crosses, a loop of tongue hung down, the legs dangled in space.

"So, in conclusion," she said, letting the drawing

flutter to the floor. "Homer is now—go on, you can guess—animal, vegetable, or mineral?"

Her crazy eyes zeroed in on us. She waited.

"Beep! Time's up," she said. "The correct answer is vegetable! If we're ever going to turn this carrot back into a prince, we need some technology!

"Yes, the rehab doctors down at Ottawa County General use something called electronic nerve stimulation to restore function to previously lifeless digits."

J-Cat gave us a broad smile and continued. "It's grueling, it's painful, and it doesn't always work, but it might just turn some of this lard into active flesh.

"Just think . . . ," she said, tapping the side of her face in an exaggerated way like I did when I was telling the crumb snatchers a story. "You could enter the gimp Olympics, maybe even push yourself across the United States with your tongue. Hey!" J-Cat jumped up and down. "It's a muscle, ain't it?"

"That's enough!" I let poor Homer's hand drop so that it hung like a rag doll's over the side of the bed. "Leave him alone!"

What was the matter with me? I wasn't paralyzed. J-Cat had invaded our turf. She'd mad-dogged me and Homer since the day we met. She didn't just lock eyes with you, she passed right through them to your brain. J-Cat didn't do her own time, she fed off the time of others.

When she saw me coming, J-Cat started to jump around like she had to pee.

"Oh, goody, goody!" she said. "A dance partner."

That day, I must have left my impulse control back at Granny's Lap. Beau always said if you think first, you lose your nerve. Whether it was smart or not, I don't know. It was happening. I wanted her like the big bad wolf wanted pig flesh, like Cinderella's ugly sisters wanted the prince. Like the Wicked Witch wanted the silver slippers, which—if you would take the time to read the book, Fish, you would know—was *the true color* of Dorothy's shoes!

J-Cat wiggled her fingers. "C'mon, Hairball," she said, "just a little closer."

I lunged. Homer screamed, "Don't!" And I tripped over the lump of rock that started it all, falling right into her spastic waiting arms.

I swear that woman must have grown up on the street. She knew how to take care of business, using my unbalanced weight against me. Before I knew it, J-Cat had me pinned in a bear hug from behind.

"Ever since I met you, I've been dying to do this," she whispered. "Now, it would help if you were relaxed, but I guess there's not much chance of that."

And right before it happened, my brain threw out strange signals. I tasted leaves after rain, felt the softness of Moonie Pie against my cheek, smelled Mr. Olatanju's cooking.

Then she cracked me.

Like an egg.

Like stomping on new ice.

There was pain at first, searing through my shoulder and down to my navel. Against the back of my eyelids, red curtains closed off the light.

And then, I had the strangest impression of water tumbling over rocks after a heavy rain, of banks overflowing with water that rushed to places it has never been.

I couldn't hold myself up. I crumpled. J-Cat lowered me to the floor. She bent my knees.

"Toss me a pillow, Homer," she said. "Oops, forgot. You're a turnip."

"God, I hate you!" Homer screamed. "What did you do to her? You'll never work again if you hurt her!"

I wanted to tell him it was all right. At least I thought it was all right.

"Let your head hang over this," she said, putting a rolled-up pillow on my knees. "Relax, Homes, you'll dislocate your tongue. I adjusted her. Her spine is so out of line it feels like a comb that's been through the garbage disposal. She's finally got blood flowing to places that have been dying of thirst."

I tried to get up, but J-Cat put a foot on my good shoulder.

"Stay," she said.

Truth be told, I didn't have much choice.

J-Cat sat down on the edge of Homer's bed. I couldn't see him, but I knew what he was doing. He was turned away from her, his head to the wall.

"Now don't be cross, Homer," she said in her annoying way. "In case you hadn't noticed—being so wrapped up in your own misery and all—your girlfriend's been in a lot of pain."

"I hate you," Homer repeated. "I hate you. I hate you. I hate you."

"Homer! Are you spitting on me? That is so clever. You know what? Before I go, I'm going to give you a present for that talented tongue of yours."

She stood up and I could see her out of the corner of my eye, her hands jammed deep into those kangaroo-pouch pockets. She grabbed a package wrapped in butcher paper that had been leaning against the wall and then all I saw were the bottoms of her tennis shoes as she climbed up on Homer's bed rail again.

I tried to push myself up one more time.

"Stay!" she ordered me. "You have to rest in that position for at least ten minutes."

I weighed my options. There was no way I could take her down now. Besides, I had other feelings to consider than how much Homer hated J-Cat. My shoulder felt warm and tingly. It wasn't sore. It wasn't throbbing. It was just . . . a shoulder.

"You okay?" I heard Homer ask.

"Yeah, thanks," I managed to say in a normal voice. "Just a little . . ."

What?

What was this feeling?

Happy?

J-Cat stapled something to the ceiling before jumping back down.

"This paper is sensitive to UV light. This penlight emits it. When you put it in your mouth like this . . ."

She kept talking but I couldn't understand her anymore. Still, if I laid my right cheek on the pillow over my knees, I could see the paper. Like magic, a line appeared on the black pad that was now stuck to the ceiling. A thin yellow line began to form into shapes that made letters and then words.

The words spelled out, *Surrender, Homer.*

"Very clever," Homer said, which meant he'd turned his head away from the wall and was looking at the words, too.

She was amazing like that. I always tried to stay away from the tough stuff with Homer. But J-Cat played right in the middle of it.

We sat there in silence as she lisped through

some stuff we couldn't understand, the pen still in her mouth. It was just a line on a piece of paper, but to Homer it must have felt like the first words that were ever written. He could draw again. He could make diagrams of new inventions, write letters, write books.

J-Cat got off the bed.

"C'mon, Hairball," she said, and helped me to my feet. I stood still as she felt her way down my arm, pressing at certain points, like she was molding it into something different.

"Now, go sit in your corner," she said. "I need room for this next trick."

And so I did, giving Homer a quick smile, seeing an expression on his face that I hadn't seen for months. He wanted that pen. He did. But he was trying his darndest not to show it.

"I figured you wouldn't want to share," she said as she licked spit off the pen she'd had in her mouth. "So I brought you one of your own and put this string around it so you could retrieve it with your bionic tongue."

As she talked, J-Cat climbed onto the rail, reached up, and tore a sheet from the pad, tucking the rest of the pages underneath a band at the bottom to keep them smooth against the backing.

"Now don't look like that," she said as she tore the sheet in her hand in two and dropped it on the floor. "There's a whole pad up here. It's big paper, so divide it into quadrants. That'll give you more drawing space."

J-Cat used her finger to divide the paper into four parts.

"I know what a quadrant is," Homer said sulkily.

"Okay, Einstein. . . ." She rubbed her hands together. "You heard the speech. So now you get your rock."

"I hauled this up from the pier myself, Homeboy, and I do hope you appreciate the effort. I pinpointed the location from the sheriff's report. Do you know they're making an informational video about the danger of diving off the Grand Haven pier since you and a couple other lunkheads took the plunge?

"That sheriff is a real sincere guy . . . feels terrible about you young boys getting turned into vegetables on his watch. I told him, 'I got just the kid to star in your film.'"

"You know what? Why don't you just shut up and go?"

"But you haven't admired the rock yet."

"I never asked you for that rock."

"Yes, that's true. But you been thinking about this rock, Homer, and don't deny it! I have my sources."

Homer and I exchanged glances. Must be Ariel

"Cheese Eater" Dinkins she was referring to. I watched all this from my corner, never really sitting down, just pressing my back and shoulders against the wall and sliding down until my knees stuck out like I was sitting on a chair. Homer's face was dry and it seemed to me he was just cranky now, wanting J-Cat to leave so he could investigate his new toy.

J-Cat let a little puff of disgust escape from the back of her throat.

"You better want this rock! Or I wasted four perfectly good hours of my life and a sundress from Value Village on this project. The sheriff oversaw it himself. I went on quite eloquently about your psycho-social factors before he agreed to drive onto the pier with his squad car and haul it out.

"That was only *after* I got arrested for trespassing, mind, but that's a whole 'nother story. . . ."

All the while she talked, J-Cat was lugging and heaving and grunting with the effort of moving this huge, wet, heavy rock. I was still tangled up in how it got into the tree house in the first place, and I couldn't imagine now how she was going to lift it up so Homer could get a good look. I wouldn't have laid a bet on her, but there she was, squatting down and heaving that rock onto the bed like one of those puffed-up weight lifters you see on TV.

My blood must have been in all the right places at that moment because when the rock hit Homer's hospital bed and made the mattress shoot up, there I was to keep him from falling into a heap on the floor.

Everything was in motion: the mattress, the rock, and Homer. For a minute, it looked like the rock was going to roll in my direction, too, giving me injuries I couldn't afford. But I held my ground for Homer, and when J-Cat corralled it to one corner of the bed, I laid him back down while he swore at her, words I'm sure I'd never heard come out of his mouth before.

She seemed completely oblivious to his words and his pain.

"These here," she said, panting and pointing at the rock, "are authentic zebra mussels . . . sharp as razors if you walk on 'em barefoot. They're what cut your face on the way down."

When I finished arranging his butterfly-light arms and legs back under the covers, Homer asked, panting, "How do I know you got the right one?"

She started tapping the side of her head. "How do you know? How do you know? Because when I was down there, I heard it bragging, that's how."

She eyeballed Homer with a look that said, *It's on, baby,* and I saw they were going to fight. Using force on a quadriplegic, that's not a fair fight, so J-Cat was going into Homer's mind. It was horrible to watch, like watching surgery on TV, but it was fascinating, too.

I didn't know how to fight like that. I would take a hit for Homer, I loved him that much. But I guess I figured, like he did, that his life—his real life—was over. My job was to be with him while he did his time.

He was down for life, wasn't he?

J-Cat didn't seem to think so.

"It's only right," she said, patting the big ugly rock, "that I leave you two alone to get acquainted. So, Homerboy, what's my next challenge? I figure I got to prove my allegiance, you know, like those knights of the Round Table.

"You asked for the rock, you got the rock."

Clearly, Homer was done playing. He was looking past her into the cold October sky and focusing his thoughts on some poor leaf, petrified of falling.

But J-Cat had not finished playing.

"Now I know you're partial to miracles, so how 'bout this. How 'bout I don't come back here until I can find someone with the same C4 injury—same break—who will dance with me? Just to prove it to you. Just to open your eyes to the possibility."

"You're serious," I said, before I thought better of it.

"Sure. We're talking miracles here, are we not? I like a good challenge."

J-Cat put on one of those mock-serious looks that makes you feel like she's taking you for a ride, bowed deep, and said: "Do me the honor, Lord Homerboy, of letting me prove my allegiance."

"Get away from me," Homer said, not loud, but in this certain way he has, like he's just invented the words.

J-Cat straightened up and asked: "Before I take my leave, may I kiss Your Lordship's big ugly toe?"

"You can bring me the dancer. Fine!" Homer spit out. "But quit playin' what's left of me for a fool. And. Don't. Touch. Me."

It was a threat Homer couldn't really make good on, so I helped out.

"Don't touch him."

J-Cat regarded us. You could be very insulting to her and she just narrowed her eyes a little with her look that said, *No speaka English.* Her fingers hovered over Homer's toe.

"If a tree falls in the middle of a forest and no one hears it, does it make a sound?" she asked, fingers inching closer.

I tensed and got ready to spring.

"If a home health aide touches the toe of a quadriplegic and no one feels it, does he still hate her?"

"Go!"

"See ya!" She kicked open the hatch and sank right through the floor.

We were alone.

Homer turned his face away from me.

He blamed me. I was his road dog, his crew, and I hadn't protected him.

It was like she put me under a spell when she cracked me like that. I tried to hate her, for his sake, but I could shrug my shoulder without it hurting for the first time in memory. I wanted to think about what she'd done and what she said. About the blood.

What if I didn't have to be in so much pain all the time?

What if Homer could draw?

I put my hand on the top of Homer's shoulder, on a spot I knew he could feel.

"It's like Hansel and Gretel," I said softly. "Both of 'em know hanging around with that witch and eating her candy is a bad idea . . . but they're starving when they get to that gingerbread house."

Homer moved his head a little, but he didn't open his eyes. He was so pale. I could see a thin vein run across the lid. When I leaned close, it pulsed faster.

"I guess when you're starving," he said, "you don't have much choice either way." Then he gave me a little smile, one side of his mouth higher up than the other, and he opened his eyes.

"How did she get that thing in here?" I asked him.

"Some guy named Stan with a cherry picker. Pushed it right through the hatch."

"You really think it's the one?"

Even with his eyes shut, Homer could raise one eyebrow and give me a look that said: *You playing me for a fool, Harry Sue?*

Finally, he opened his eyes.

"My feeling is this: The rock was not my finest idea. But I can think of a thing or two to do with that pen."

Chapter 24

"As long as we are in here, enjoying a meal together, it would be fine for you to call me Baba," Mr. Olatanju said the next day as I wrestled with his name.

He was unpacking something from a cooler. Just the smell made the back of my mouth tingle.

"It means that we are friends. That is what my friends call me." He looked up at me and smiled, just for a moment, before busying himself again with his meal.

"That is what they *called* me. Where I came from."

"Maybe here," I said. "But not always."

I tried to imagine what Jolly Roger and his associates would do with the information that I was friends with the art teacher. It wouldn't be safe for Mr. Ola . . . it wouldn't be safe for Baba.

"Of course," Baba was saying as he pulled plates out of a basket. "I understand. We create something together when we are here. And it doesn't exist anywhere else. And when we are not here, it doesn't exist in this room, either."

He unfolded my napkin with a snap before handing it to me. "It is only present when we are present."

I set down my backpack and unzipped it. "You got me thinking about a story, Mr. . . . Baba," I said. "You ever heard of *The Wizard of Oz*?"

"I have seen that movie. It is about the girl . . . Dorothy?"

Oh, brother.

"But before it was a movie, it was a book. The book is the real story. And there's a wizard in it. But he's not really a wizard. He just starts playing all the Munchkins . . . and he does it for so long, they *think* he's for real."

I pulled Oswald out of my backpack and fished around in the bottom for his missing eye.

"Nothing is the way it's supposed to be in that place," I said. "But even after he gets busted, it's like he can still fix things. He's not magic, but he can still make all their dreams come true . . . well, except for Dorothy, but she's a special case."

I stopped, feeling out of breath. I wasn't used to

talking about this stuff with anybody but Homer. And this idea that was in my head was slapping me around.

"Okay." I decided to try again. "It's like he set up Oz to work a certain way, but then when Toto knocks over the screen and everybody sees he's just a little old man and not a big powerful wizard, he makes this great recovery. I mean, he loses 'em when he gets caught. And the Scarecrow calls him a humbug—which was a real insult in Oz—but then—just with words!—he pulls them back. . . ."

I fell back in my chair, exhausted. I couldn't get it right, what I was trying to say. I wanted to tell Baba that I understood what he said about making a home just for a minute with words and food, knowing all the while it couldn't last forever. It could only be real for a short time.

But I wasn't sure how to say all that, so I held on to my tongue and put the bear on the table.

"Can you fix this?"

Baba reached out slowly and took Carly Mae's precious bear into his big hands, giving me another chance to admire Granny's handiwork. Oswald's ear was nearly torn off, and the piece of yarn that was his mouth hung in a string. His plump tummy had gone flat, as if she'd beaten all the cheerfulness out of him.

"I figured since you're an art teacher and all . . ."

"A substitute, remember? In the art classroom."

Baba turned the little bear over. "He has met with an accident, no?"

I nodded. "It's Carly Mae's. She's one of the crum . . . the little kids at Granny's Lap."

"Yes, I can fix him." He laid the bear down carefully, next to the serving dishes. "But first, I want you to do something for me, Harry Sue."

Har-ee Sue.

There was something about him today. Quieter. Slower. He left the covered dishes where they were and began pulling squeeze bottles of paint off the shelves. Red, yellow, purple, blue. He set them in front of me along with a big metal cookie sheet.

I looked at Baba, waiting.

"Will you paint with me, Harry Sue?"

"Paint with you?"

"My wife tells me that to heal we need to go back to the time before it happened, back to when we still painted with our fingers."

I wasn't sure what he was on about, but he looked so serious as he set another cookie sheet next to mine and squirted red paint onto it that I picked up the blue paint bottle. After blue, I squirted yellow right on top of it. Swirling my fingers in the paint, I made streaks of green appear from the other two colors.

I looked up at Baba. Was this what he wanted?

He put blue on top of his red and moved his fingers until they swirled purple.

I tried to remember before, but I couldn't. I tried to, for Baba's sake, but I'd laid too many pictures down after, pictures of how things would be after Mary Bell came back. They were on top of the old pictures—the real pictures. I couldn't get to those anymore.

So instead I painted the way Baba's food felt inside me . . . the food I was smelling at that very moment: tomatoes, lamb, peppers, spices. All the different things—the vegetables, the meat, the fruit—became one thing, one big green growing thing, like the runner beans that crawled up the back of Mrs. Mead's garage.

And Baba made one thing, too, but all his colors became a muddy brown, like the shallow ponds that suddenly appear when the swamp overflows.

After a few minutes, he collected our sheets and put them in the big sink at the back of the room and ran water over them. Then they were just cookie sheets again. Because of the paint, we washed our hands in the sink and didn't use the penny bowl and the pitcher. I wanted to, anyway, just to feel the cool water running over my hands, but I didn't ask.

As we began to eat, I tried to put all my bad thoughts of what Granny had done to Carly Mae's bear into a cupboard so they didn't spoil the taste of the food.

"You have to go back, too?" I asked him. "To the time before?"

He looked up at me. In the joint, if somebody looks you in the eye after you ask a personal question, that means it's okay to go ahead. So I did.

"Was that in Africa?"

"Sudan," he said, nodding. He pulled a fat little banana from a bunch in his basket and cut the stem with an exacto knife.

"So that's home?"

"The country is there, yes," he said, chewing slowly. "We can find it on a map. But the village where I was born and where I was a young boy is gone. My family . . . all gone: my two brothers, my parents, my uncle Aboduin . . ."

Baba set the dishes in front of us on the table and unwrapped the bread. He took off the lids, and I felt like even if all I could eat were those smells, I would be happy.

"There was a civil war. . . . The soldiers came to our village and burned everything. They killed everyone. When the soldiers came, my mother told me to run. I was a very fast runner. I ran very fast and I hid. But when I came back, everything was gone. . . ."

It seemed wrong to eat while Baba was talking about such things, but he set out the plates and placed a round fat pancake on each one. Taking the covers off of the dishes, he waited for me to begin. He wouldn't talk again unless I was eating. I took a deep breath and tore off a piece of my pancake.

"There were a few other boys like me, who were left with nothing. There was nothing to do but leave our village. And so we began to walk. We walked because there was no reason to stay. And we were hungry. We didn't know where we were going, and after a while, we didn't know where we were.

"Walking was very dangerous, Harry Sue. Some of the boys were killed by lions. One was eaten by a crocodile as we crossed a river. And there were the patrols.

"I was much afraid to be so lost. But we knew that to be found could be even worse. If the soldiers found us . . . We had to keep going and trust. It was the fear that kept us moving night and day. Finally we arrived at a refugee camp. There were so many children, thousands, just like us. Most of them were boys. That is why they called us the 'Lost Boys.'"

Even though Baba hadn't eaten anything but the little banana, he pushed his plate aside and picked up Oswald. I shoved food into my mouth and smiled, wanting to make him happy again.

Baba went to the teacher's desk and pulled out a small plastic case filled with needles and spools of thread and a tiny scissors. He came back and sat down again.

I tore off another piece of my bread and held it over a pot of creamy sauce with pieces of chicken floating in it.

"But how did you get here?" I asked him, dunking my bread and pinching the chicken.

"That's very good," he said, as I held it up for him to see.

He squinted, threading the needle.

"There is an Episcopal church in Marshfield. Many churches in your country have brought Lost Boys to America. I was one of the first boys to come. I have been here now for almost eight years."

Baba took a piece of napkin and wiped the exacto knife clean. Then he held up Oswald and inserted the knife into his back, razoring him open at the seam.

He got up again and walked to a cupboard at the back of the room. When he returned, he had a bag of cotton balls. By the way he walked, with his shoulders hunched, I could see that telling this story was like making me relive my fall.

Soon as I knew that, I stopped even wanting to ask.

"This is really good," I said. "Do you cook all this, or does your wife cook, too?"

He tore open the bag of cotton balls and laughed. "My wife cannot cook," he said. "Or maybe I should say, we cannot eat her cooking. I am the cook in the family." He set a handful of cotton balls on the table and looked at me. "You see, Harry Sue, in my country it is not the men who cook. But since this food makes such a . . . such a pleasant memory, I decided to learn."

"Do your kids like this food as much as I do?"

My guess was that Baba didn't have any kids, but how could I be sure? I didn't want him to have any, I knew that, and if I'd been my old self, it would have worried me to know I was getting so attached. But now, with the letters and everything, well, I was throwing caution to the wind.

Baba focused his concentration on Oswald again, inserting one cotton ball after the other and pushing them around inside the bear's tummy with his thumbs.

"We cannot have children," he said. "She was very sick when she was younger and the medicine they used to treat her made her sterile."

What the heck was "sterile"? I thought it meant clean, but clearly it meant you couldn't have kids, too. That must have made Baba really, really sad. He lost his family and he couldn't make a new one.

"Sorry," I said, swallowing. I thought he might cry after telling me all that, so I kept my head down out of respect.

"You don't have to be sorry, Harry Sue. But let us talk of happier things, no? Do you think your friend would like it if I gave her bear a nice necktie to wear to church on Sunday?"

The rest of the time, he worked in silence. As he

was knotting the last thread, Baba said: "You must remember, Harry Sue. Where I come from, no one is ever really lost to us. Not as long as you hold them in the palm of your heart."

He smiled at me so sadly then that I wasn't sure if I should say anything or not. I decided not. I thought maybe a look would be good, but the current Harry Sue catalog of looks did not contain an item for this moment.

Before I came, I had been thinking of telling Baba about the letters. But watching his face when he wasn't looking changed my mind.

I didn't want him to know how close I was to being found.

At that moment, I just wanted to stay lost with him.

Part 4
Courage

"You have plenty of courage, I am sure," answered Oz. "All you need is confidence in yourself. There is no living thing that is not afraid when it faces danger. True courage is in facing danger when you are afraid, and that kind of courage you have in plenty."

"Perhaps I have, but I'm scared just the same," said the Lion. "I shall really be very unhappy unless you give me the sort of courage that makes one forget he is afraid."

—*The Wizard of Oz*

Chapter 25

I walked home that day, my mind full of the things that Baba told me. His story weighed me down and made my shoulders ache with sympathy. But what pulled me up was that I was going to put my hands on places where Mary Bell had put her hands. I was going to hold her in the palm of my heart, like Baba said, and we'd take up the book on the page we'd left off the night Garnett blew through the door and I went out the window and he and Mary Bell got sent up. It was the place where the Wicked Witch makes Dorothy her slave, and she can't run away because the Lion is being held prisoner. Me and Mary Bell were finally going to get past the part where things looked the worst for old Dorothy.

Even the smell of wet smoke didn't trouble my dreams. After all, it was the time of year for burning leaves.

"Where is she?" I asked when I got to the kitchen, pulling out the smoochy girl I'd retrieved from her dried grass nest and unwrapping her from her half-roll of toilet paper.

"Out back," Sink said, avoiding my eyes.

"The kids?"

"In the basement watching a show."

"Moonie Pie?"

"Where do you think?"

So I shrugged off my backpack and went outside to tell the old bat it was time to deal.

Granny burned leaves in a big can made out of wire mesh so even the leaves at the bottom would get air. She stood there, squinting into the smoke, her cigar in one hand and a single envelope in the other.

I wasn't used to looking her in the eye, but I wasn't about to back down now. Not even when she gave me her look that said, *It's on!*

"Wish I could tell ya that you got a letter from your old Mary Hag, but it just ain't true. You never did."

"What's that, then?" I asked. I wasn't even troubled. Lying was like breathing to Granny.

"Even when I try to starve it out, you look more like her every day," she said, shaking her head. "Never could stand that woman. Didn't trust her."

Granny narrowed her eyes at me. "Dark as a gypsy, that one. She sure did put it over on my Garnett. Made him plumb crazy. . . . Forgot all his dreams. He was gonna be designing cars, not putting mirrors in 'em on a factory line."

Much as I enjoyed going down memory lane with Granny, I wanted that letter even more. I started walking toward her real slow, smoochy girl perched in my outstretched hand.

"And when I burn it," she said, "all bets are off. Go on and break what you got. There's a number on the bottom to reorder."

"Give me my letter, you old . . ."

Granny poked at the fire with her stick. Her bloodshot eyes watered as she locked her stare on me through the smoke. "You're slow, girl. It is *not* your letter."

"You got no right to keep it."

But Granny dropped the letter on the smoking pile anyway, and that's when I felt Clotkin blood rushing to places it had never been before. Growling, I jumped at her and rattled the wire cage, looking for my letter. But that smoke was blinding. So I pushed the can over with all my might, hoping to save it. I pushed it right at Granny, hoping against hope that something hot and glowing would scar her forever the way she had scarred me.

She screamed and jumped back, falling to the ground as the ashes hit her.

"See what you done!" There she was, rolling on the ground, beating at the piles of gray ash that had landed on her and around her. I threw myself down, too, searching for the letter but closing my hands instead on a broken piece of smoochy girl.

"You'll go to jail for this, see if you won't," Granny cried.

But I didn't pay her any mind because I saw it then, lifting gently on the hot air. Just out of my reach. Out of Granny's, too. I scrambled to my feet and took off after it, feeling like Dorothy must have felt with the balloon just beyond her fingers, feeling just like Dorothy that this was my only way home.

Chapter 26

Baba's house wasn't far from Granny's, maybe a quarter mile, but in the strange way of our neighborhood, I don't remember ever seeing it before. It sat almost directly behind another, bigger house with only two narrow tracks to make up the driveway.

I never was afraid of the night or being out in it. As you have learned by now, Fish, people were my main problem. But tonight I felt so crazy I was shivering, and in looking for some safe place to settle, I thought of here. *Baba's tires drove here*, I told myself, putting one foot in front of the other. I had my backpack on my shoulder, and it was filled with cold ashes. Buried inside were the pretties I'd scored off

Granny as well as Granny's letter from Garnett, for safekeeping.

Dorothy never made it to the balloon, but I caught up with the letter, just as it was settling onto the surface of the swamp out back. Splashing in, I nabbed it, never giving one thought to how I would smell later. Lifting the flap, I read what I could, icy cold water pinching my toes.

It wasn't a long letter, just a single sheet, and even though it was burned, I could make out most of it. It was from my father, Garnett Clotkin, dated not long after he was sent up north to the state correctional facility for men.

Dear Ma, well you always said I would come to know good and now sending you a letter from the joint. You can go on and sell the car and spend that money on what you need for Harry Sue. . . .

There were other things he wanted her to sell so she could take care of me. Things I never knew about to get money I never saw.

Garnett wasn't much of a writer. He came to the point quick.

I swear to God, Ma, if you touch one hair on her head, I'll never speak to you again. That child is the only good ever come of Garnett Clotkin and when I get out, I'm gone take care of her real good. Now if anything happens to me or Mary Bell, you got to promise not to hurt her. Don't you ever do them things you did to me. . . .

Granny was right. It wasn't my letter.

By the time I reached Baba's house, I could feel the fatigue crawling up my aching shoulders to sit there like a winged monkey.

Granny always drew the curtains. She didn't want strangers to know we had no man in the house. But the picture window at Baba's was completely bare. With the room lit up, it looked like the stage at the Cherry Creek Playhouse in Marshfield, where every fourth grader at Trench Vista goes to see a matinee to get some culture. Looking through that window was more interesting to me than any play in the whole world even though there was only one lamp, an overstuffed chair, and a worn-out rug on the floor.

This was the home of Baba, where strange fruits and chunks of meat and spices got mixed together, where he cleaned out the clay from under his fingernails, where he tossed and turned in bed after waking from a nightmare about real lions, not some lame movie lion who was just a buster in a cat suit.

What I wanted to do was sit outside his window until he walked into the room. I wanted to watch him turn out the light.

But instead, I went on searching.

The light from the living room had given me a little strength, but when I turned away, that strength poured out of me, like emptying a glass of water onto the ground. I was so tired. The backyard was dark and cold. Every once in a while, the clouds would move and a little light would fall on the ground, but otherwise I had to make my way in the dark.

Baba took care of things. That was clear. There were still flowers, even though it was October, and there was shredded stuff in the flower beds to keep out the weeds.

I was going to grow stuff, too, someday, after I found Mary Bell and we got sprung. I liked flowers. Not those stupid cheerful all-day flowers, like daisies, that reminded me of teachers who smiled no matter what, even when they were boiling mad.

I liked big flowers, like poppies, that held secrets inside them. You can't cut a poppy and stick it in a vase. It just shrivels right up. You gotta leave poppies alone.

If you'd read the book, you would know that it was poppies that put Dorothy to sleep, not those stupid plastic flowers they made in some factory out in California and waved all over that stupid movie set. But even so, I liked poppies.

Or those other ones that make such a fuss out of their own petals, any wind can knock them over. They just lie on the ground, like Homer, helpless, but still beautiful. Mrs. Mead grew those flowers next door. You watched the buds getting fat for weeks, then right when they should bloom, they lie on the ground like they don't care for living at all.

My teeth started to chatter and I had to push

that mess about flowers out of my mind and concentrate. At the back of the little garden was a shed with the door held closed by a latch. When I lifted it, the door swung away, banging against the side. I was too tired to jump at the noise. I stepped inside, letting my eyes get used to an even darker darkness. There were sacks of things along the wall and big clay flowerpots stacked upside down in a tall tower near the door.

He wouldn't need those until spring, would he? I set down my backpack and pried the pots apart. That's where I set the letter. Then I fished around in the cold ashes of my backpack for the pieces of smoochy girl, the squirrel, the four-fingered princess, and the peasant boy. When I'd laid them on the ground, I stuck my hand in one of the sacks along the wall. Inside, it felt smooth and cold. Sand. I put Granny's pretties in the bag of sand. Maybe Baba would fill a hole in the spring with this sand and a china tree would grow from the nut held between the squirrel's paws.

After I closed up the bag, there was nothing left to do but surrender my mind to the real reason I was there, Fish. Not that you'll ever be bumpin' your gums about it. Drop a dime on Harry Sue and live to regret it.

I sat down on the floor of Baba's shed, put my empty backpack against my face, and started to cry. You know the sort of cry where you're afraid your insides will leak out? Where your stomach's pushing so hard, you wonder if it will jump into your throat and make you choke on it? Well, I cried like that in Baba's shed.

And I knew then why I had found my way to this place, putting my hands in the very same places where Baba put his hands. Because I had to let the thought approach my mind that maybe there never were any letters from Mary Bell, Fish. It was possible that Mary Bell had forgotten all about me.

After I'd wiped the snot and the tears off my face, I dragged myself back around to the front of the house, where I saw another light had been turned on in the hall. Baba stood at the door, looking out into the darkness as if searching. I don't think he heard me and I was sure he hadn't seen me because I hid back in the bushes. He was looking for something else, something that wasn't there, like Dorothy searching for Aunt Em's face in the land of the Munchkins.

He pressed one big cream-colored palm to the window. I was frozen. Waiting. Finally he gave up looking for something out there and moved to the chair in the front room. A piece of bright-colored material was draped over one arm of the chair and Baba picked it up as he sat, pressing it between his fingers, as if what he might be looking for was hiding in the threads.

Then suddenly, he was attacked from behind by

a blur of fabric and red, red hair. Thrown forward onto the ground, they wrestled together, and I was just about to forget myself again and bust up the front door in a rush to protect him when it hit me like a sucker punch.

Baba was rolling on the floor with J-Cat. They weren't wrestling, they were hugging each other. Baba put his head on her shoulder and she stroked his ear slowly. They sat on the floor, her crazy flowered dress spread in front of her, spread over both of them, and she looked at the piece of cloth that he was holding.

He wiped his eyes quickly, like he was wiping away sweat, but I know he was crying, Fish.

That's the kind of secret that we shared.

As I turned to go, I saw J-Cat's orange Volvo in the pool of porch light that spilled into the garage.

On the way home, it started to rain again.

Chapter 27

Imagine you've been sentenced to an all day, Fish. You're retired. And you've only done an eight ball. You wake up one morning, knowing you'll only ever see the sun rise through loops of razor-sharp ribbon wire. That's a place no conette ever wants to go. Why? Because it's the last stop before the ding wing, that's why. When you're faced with life in prison and you're not even close to checking out, you've got to find yourself some coping skills.

As you have probably observed, Fish, coping is my middle name. When those thoughts occurred to me about Mary Bell, I did what the lifers do. I tried to think of something else. I started singing old songs in my head. I picked the lock on the cash box in Granny's bedroom and conned Ariel Dinkins into a ride to Harvey's Home Improvement Center to score a safety gate. I put those thoughts of Mary Bell in a cupboard with Carly Mae's busted bear and I moved along.

"Okay, pick up the phone," Homer said next day when I stopped in after detention. "I memorized the number."

"That lady doesn't want to talk to us, Homes. I'm not calling."

"Sure, Consuela wants to talk to us." He looked pale. Even though it was getting colder, Homer still spent part of every day in his tree house. His hands felt like ice.

"I've talked to her three times since you did," he said, looking very satisfied with himself. "All the conettes there know me."

"Who's been dialing then?" I asked, trying to sound like it didn't matter.

"Recently, Mrs. Dinkins and I have been spending more quality time together," Homer answered matter-of-factly, as if that wasn't news.

"*She's* been coming up here?"

Homer gave me his "and you were born . . . ?" look.

"Look, Harry Sue. I'm not the only gimp to exist on the planet, and you're not the only conette kid who's lost her mother. Consuela doesn't have kids, but her super has two and there's a 'no contact' rule between them, mostly due to the fact that Alicia tried to hire an undercover cop to off her husband."

"What are you on about?"

"They're rooting for you, dog. There's nothing more important than blood to a conette."

"So?"

"So what's the matter with you, Harry Sue? You're awful funny today. Seems to me like the closer we get to finding—"

I put my fingers to Homer's lips to quiet him. At that moment, all I wanted to do was put grass under my feet. But you can't walk away from a conversation in a tree house.

I forced myself to look Homer in the eye and *focus!* as thoughts banged on the other side of the cupboard, trying to get out.

"I'm afraid, Homes," I whispered. "Afraid Mary Bell doesn't want to be found."

He was already mad that I put my fingers on his mouth. Shutting him up was a serious sign of disrespect. But now he was even madder.

"I say you're off your nut, Harry Sue. You're not afraid she doesn't want you. You're afraid you don't want her."

Homer had gone too far. I stepped back from his bed, almost tripping over the big crusty rock that J-Cat had brought back from Grand Haven and now took up most of the floor space that was left.

"Because when you two do connect, that's what will be for real."

"And you're the one who knows what's for real? Up here? In slam down?"

"Why don't you be honest, Harry Sue? I know why I'm here."

"Okay, then. Be honest. Give it to me. Why are you here instead of down there?" *With her.*

We were fighting. We were landing invisible blows. What was it Beau said about wounding with words? I didn't want to fight with Homer. I wanted to back down.

"Let's stop, Homer," I said. I was pleading with him. *Before we go too far.*

"We can't stop, Harry Sue. Just like you can't keep Mary Bell up there in your mind forever. She's gonna get sprung, dog. Sooner or later, she's gonna get sprung."

"And I *do so* want to be there." I folded my arms and turned to the wall.

"I know you do." Homer sighed a long sigh. "Okay?"

I didn't answer him, but he tried to rally anyway, tried to pull us back.

"So Alicia knows a line hack in R and D. She promised to ask her. That's why we have to call today. Mrs. Dinkins says she'll dial if you lose your nerve."

I tried to picture Mrs. Dinkins with an outside interest. It was a whole new game. Reuniting me and Mary Bell might be like getting the golden cap with the diamond and rubies on it that controlled the winged monkeys. Maybe the only way out of the hole she was in because of Homer was to do what the Good Witch did when she got the cap, and use her wishes to make everybody else's dreams come true.

It was all too much to take standing up. I couldn't be mad at Homer. Using his rock for a step, I climbed onto the bed and looked up at the little black pad with the shaky outlines of leaves he'd drawn, wondering who had been tearing off the pages for him. I knew I had no right to the information. It was Homer's cell and Homer's time.

Let Homer do his own time.

I tried to slow my breathing to his. "They look just like leaves," I said.

"But they're not. They're not anything."

"How can they not be anything?"

"Mrs. Dinkins checked out a book on Matisse from the library for me."

I pushed myself up onto my elbows. "For real, Homes. Has she been up here?"

"Nah, she's got to yoke up before she can do that."

There were sounds in the driveway, like more

than one vehicle was pulling in to park. Major sounds.

"J-Cat?"

"Can't be," Homer said. "She's got to bring me that miracle, remember?"

But the sounds continued. At first, it was the same electric sound that Homer's bed made when it was being raised.

"There's something real wrong about her," I said, resisting the urge to pull up the hatch and check it out . . . resisting the image in my mind of J-Cat the other night, holding Baba in her arms.

"You think come winter she'll put on a pair of pants?"

A loud smack shook the tree house. Instinctively, I rolled away from it toward the center of the bed. Homer's body rolled in my direction.

Then the sound of J-Cat's voice calling, "Stan! I marked it right between those lines."

A man's voice answering: "Gotcha." The sound of a machine starting up. "All clear?"

"What's going on?" Homer screamed over the drone. I put my arms around him and held his head, protecting him from I don't know what.

As if to answer the question that was right in the front of our minds, a chain saw sliced through the side of Homer's tree house at exactly the same moment J-Cat pulled herself up through the hatch.

"No need to panic!" she called out over the noise. "Just a little remodeling."

"Just *what* do you think you are doing to my house?!"

Homer was yelling about as loud as he could, but he couldn't compete with the noise of the buzz saw. He kept yelling himself hoarse until it sputtered to an end and a square the size of a Monopoly board fell out of the side of his tree house. A rush of cold air replaced it and then the head of Stan.

"I repeat . . . ," Homer said. "What do you think you're doing?"

"Now, don't spit in my face, Homerboy," J-Cat dished back. "Technically, this structure belongs to one Ariel Dinkins, and I've got a permit." She held up a piece of paper with what looked like a child's crayon drawing of the tree house. Only in addition to the skylight in the roof, there was a window down near the floor.

"With this new window, you'll have a bird's-eye view of the underworld."

I looked at the hole. Stan was now working away at the edges with a big file, sending wood shavings all over the place, and putting a level on the line to see if it balanced. Behind him, I could see Homer's house and the kitchen window where his mother stationed herself 24-7.

"Before the window goes in, I got something to

show you," J-Cat said, swooshing her big fabric tulips around the bed and hopping on.

"Got it hooked up to that winch, Stan?"

"Check," Stan said, and went back to his filing.

"Hand me that rope, Hairball, and make yourself useful."

I looked hard at J-Cat, trying to figure out what Baba might see in her. I didn't think too much that way—you know, romantically. Far as I could tell, it didn't lead anywhere good.

I mean, look at my mom and dad. Look at the Tin Man.

But loving J-Cat . . . that was just, well, Category J.

And at that moment, I was less into whatever new rock she wanted to hoist into Homer's tree house than I was his new view. It made me think about the two of them—Homes and his mom—in a whole new way. Lying there, looking down, I realized that Mrs. Dinkins had lost a child just like I had lost a mother. Homer was too wrapped up in his own self to notice the mother always searching the sky for him.

Or, maybe, she wasn't the mother he wanted to find.

But J-Cat noticed. And she was trying to bring them back together.

I got down off the bed and took the rope that Stan had tossed through the opening.

"I got a dancer on the end of this line, just like I promised, Homer. You'll see." J-Cat gritted her teeth. "Pull," she barked at me, and, hand over hand, we hauled up whatever was on the end of that rope.

"Get out of the way, Stan!" she yelled. "These things are heavy."

Stan's head disappeared out of sight and suddenly I could see Mrs. Dinkins clear as day down below. She stood down there, hugging herself and shivering, her worry just like rays of light.

I glanced over at Homer, who had stalked out of the room in his mind. He was turned to the wall, away from the hole Stan had cut through and away from J-Cat, whose legs were braced against the pull on the end of the line.

"Get ready to haul her in, Hairball," she said as a television set came into view, suspended in midair, wrapped all around in ropes like an old sea chest.

"Help me out here," J-Cat grunted. "I'll hold."

A cord dangled from the bottom of the set and I lay flat on my stomach as I reached through the hole to grab it and guide it in. A long orange extension cord was attached to the TV cord, and I followed it with my eyes as it swayed all the way down to the little silver cap that covered the outlet on the outside of the Dinkinses' house.

It shocked me with a memory of Mr. Dinkins,

standing there in a Santa cap, making me and Homer climb this very tree and tell him how the lights looked from above.

He didn't tell us that he'd set down the lights like a landing strip, heading straight for the chimney.

"Old Santa's not going to have any trouble with this one," Homer had said, punching me. Only that was when he was still Christopher.

"You think he'll bring my presents here again?" I asked.

Mr. Dinkins told me that Santa got all confused with Granny's home being a day care but me living there all the time.

"Some reason or another, he's got the crazy idea you live with us, Harry Sue," he'd said, taking off his Santa cap and scratching his bald head. "Well, I don't suppose it's much of a problem to pass on your gifts. . . ."

I got good presents right up until Homer dove himself off the Grand Haven pier.

The memory of it all was like electricity coursing through my arm and I almost didn't have the sense to get out of the way as J-Cat performed her sumo-wrestling move to get the TV onto the bed.

It wasn't just a plain old TV set. It had a slot for a DVD at the bottom.

"Now, Homer," she said, pressing the power button and ejecting the DVD that was already inside. "I know you're mad at me. And you got a right. But I was mad first, see?

"Why? Because you don't honor your mother, that's why. I don't know nuts about your father, but your mother is right downstairs, in a manner of speaking."

Homer kept his face turned to the wall.

"So in addition to your miracle, I got another present for you, Homeboy. And I'm going to speak plain. My goal is to get you out of this tree. I admit it! And this window here is to remind you there's a whole 'nother world you been missing.

"Your goal is to stay up here in a cocoon. Fair enough. But," she continued, pulling a remote control out of her pocket, "you've at least got to make an informed choice."

J-Cat examined the DVD for fingerprints, rubbing it hard on her thigh before she pushed it back into the slot. The set wobbled dangerously on the wadded-up covers at the foot of the bed.

"So here's your present. Stan's not just going to put in a window," she said, "he's going to insulate your little hideaway, and I got an old ceramic heater we can stick up here that'll make you as snug as a piece of toast in a toaster all winter long. Of course, the heat'll fog up the windows and you'll feel like you're floating inside a cloud, but something tells me you got the idea that would be Homer heaven."

Slowly, Homer brought his head around to face J-Cat. He glared.

"Sometimes I think about hurting you real bad," he said, his voice still hoarse.

"I'd like that." She was smiling. "I'd really, really like that.

"Maybe you could get Hairball here to saw on the rope so it breaks when I'm trying to climb up. Or maybe when I'm reattaching my TV set to the winch, she can push me out of that hole. . . . Well, it'll be a window by then. But if she's clever—"

J-Cat broke off and looked me up and down.

"You know what you need, Homer? You need some new henchmen. You ever notice how ineffective Hairball is? She couldn't scare the pants off a duckling.

"How's the shoulder, by the way?" she asked, turning her attention toward me. "I don't suppose you'd let me . . ."

J-Cat wiggled her fingers at me. I glanced over at Homer. He was giving her the death stare. I gave it to her, too, even though my whole body ached to be cracked by J-Cat one more time.

"I don't see any dancers," Homer was saying through clenched teeth. "You weren't supposed to come back until . . ."

"Oh, he's here," J-Cat said, sticking the DVD into the slot. "He's right here. And so, without further ado . . ." She checked to see that the cord was still plugged into the back of the set and pressed the "play" button.

You could tell right away we were in a home movie. The camera operator was not real steady and the way the picture swayed and the television, too, I felt a little seasick.

"This place is swank," the guy with the camera was saying to himself. "Check out the garden . . . Okay, okay, but just one." The camera, which had been focused on a dusky garden with stone benches and a tall green hedge, dipped down as we heard the sound of a match striking cement and then someone inhaling.

"That's better. . . . Now check out them roses." He panned over to a wall of pure white blossoms, their faces shining in the pale light. "I could maybe live here," he said, sucking again on the cigarette.

"Marty! Would you get your sorry butt in here! You already missed Anna throwing her bouquet. She nailed Granny Perkins."

"Crap!" Marty said. We heard the sound of his shoe scratching out the cigarette and were forced to jog back inside with Marty, the camera bobbling all over the place. He made his way through a kitchen and then a set of double doors when suddenly, everything went dark.

I glanced over at J-Cat. She was completely absorbed, just like the crumb snatchers when they're watching a good TV program.

"Marty's gonna be late for his own funeral," she said to the TV.

The ballroom was dim and as the camera adjusted to the light, I could just make out the people: their shiny shoes, their shimmering pearls, tuxedos, long dresses. They stood in a circle, talking quietly and pressing their hands together.

Marty focused on an old man with a microphone.

"Now Danny Boy will have the first dance with his new bride to the heavenly sounds of 'Some Enchanted Evening.'"

"This is it!" J-Cat said, punching me on the arm. "Don't blame me if I cry. I always cry at weddings."

There was a moment of silence, then an electric noise that I thought at first was the camera.

But it wasn't. It was a wheelchair.

Marty whistled "Here Comes the Bride" as something strange wheeled into the dim light. It took me a while to see that it was two people, a man in a wheelchair with a woman in a huge wedding dress in his lap. You could hardly see him the way her dress hung over them both. She was hugging him so tight, her arms locked around his neck the way that Moonie Pie latched on to me when I let him. Her legs were tucked up so they wouldn't get in the way of the wheels.

The sound of a whole orchestra swelled up in the background and the chair started to move, not like some mechanical thing, but like something real. Something alive.

It swayed back and forth the way I've seen people do who are slow dancing.

I guess we all knew who the bride was. Hard to mistake the hair. Still, when J-Cat looked into the camera and smiled, I heard Homer suck in his breath.

She was wedged between us now, her eyes locked onto the screen.

"Some enchanted evening . . . ," she sang in a scratchy voice, reaching up and pulling the television closer to us.

It was really impressive the way he could move that wheelchair. Now it was making lazy circles around the edge of the dance floor. J-Cat picked up the hem of her dress, all dainty, and waved it as they sailed across the floor.

All the faces they whirled past seemed so happy, like a little light went on inside each one as the wedding couple passed. Marty was getting better with the camera and we saw the groom's face a couple of times, pressed against his headrest, laughing, stealing a kiss from J-Cat's cheek.

It was just like in the story. When you get to Oz, you have to put on the green glasses. They make everything perfect. Nobody seemed to notice that the guy couldn't put out an arm to catch her if she fell. They didn't notice that he had wheels instead of legs. The happiness of the two people in that wheelchair was the green glass making everything perfect.

". . . you will meet a stranger. He will be stranger . . . than anyone you've ever seen. . . ."

I stole a look at J-Cat. Tears were streaming down her cheeks.

She picked up the remote and froze the picture. "You see, Homerboy," she said, tapping a grubby finger on the screen. "You think you can't feel anything, but you can. You can feel love. But right now your fear is weighing you down, like a big ugly blanket. It's smothering you, Homes. It's the bushel over your light."

"Where is he now?" I asked, thinking of the other night, of J-Cat and Baba.

J-Cat stared at me with a look I couldn't figure. At first, I thought she was scared. But then I knew I guessed wrong when she burst into a fresh round of tears and threw her arms around the television set.

"He's dead," she said, sobbing as if her heart would break open right there, as if underneath all that craziness she was as soft as me.

We stayed quiet while she cried, the whole bed shaking with her grief.

Finally, she stopped and yanked on the hem of

her sundress, rubbing it all over her face before using it to wipe her nose.

J-Cat looked at Homer and said, "He's dead, Homer. But before he died . . . he lived."

She rubbed at her eyes like a tired kid and hiccuped.

"If you'd just try . . . just a little . . . it wouldn't seem like he was so dead."

Chapter 28

The only time I get to think is on my way to and from school. At Granny's, you've always got to watch your back. I even know how to sleep with my eyes open. It's good practice for the joint if you have a mind to go.

Which I don't anymore. Sorry, Fish. We've done hard time together. But now it's time for me to get sprung.

And the first rule for life after the joint is this: Everything's always changing. Prepare to be surprised.

It was hard to know how to feel about it all. I mean, there went all my career plans. Up in smoke.

Like my belief in Mary Bell's letters.

Like the leaves Homer willed to jump into Granny's burn pile.

I always thought learning to be tough would be just as helpful on the outs, but J-Cat had me all messed up about that. Her big thing was opening up, even if it felt like taking a sucker punch to the heart.

What I really couldn't figure was what she had left over for Baba. After I saw how sad she felt about Danny, I replayed what I'd seen the night before. I mean, there was no way another lady could step in and be Mary Bell, was there? How could you love two people that strong?

For some reason, it didn't hurt so much to remember her comforting Baba.

Jeez, maybe I saw it all wrong. Maybe he was the one comforting her.

"Harry Sue! A word." Mr. Hernandez put a hand on my shoulder as I took my place lining up for class. He was winded, and his tie had flapped over his shoulder. For some reason, the smell was really bad today, like a load of plugged-up toilets had been dumped in the yard.

Mr. Hernandez put his tie over his mouth as he spoke.

"The Marshfield EMS wants to honor you at a special ceremony this afternoon down at the Fire Station," he said, trying to catch his breath and not breathe in the fumes at the same time.

I looked at him, so surprised I forgot my catalog of looks altogether.

He looked at me, too, like he was seeing me for the first time: my faded white painter's pants, the T-shirt with the rip in the sleeve, my shoes two sizes too big.

"Reporters are going to be there," he said. "That the best you got?"

"These are my Sunday clothes," I said, conjuring up a pretty lame "mad but dumb." "Doesn't matter anyway. I got detention today."

I put my hands on my hips, trying to cover a purple Kool-Aid stain.

"Tell 'em thanks, though."

"Oh, you can make it, Harry Sue. I'll excuse you from detention *and* I'll drive you. The mayor's looking for more good news out of the public schools and, like I said, they've got a photographer coming and everything. What about your grandma? Don't suppose she could find it in her heart to be there?"

"She would have to *have* a heart," I said, "to be able to find it."

I did not cover for Granny. She wasn't my road dog.

Mr. Hernandez didn't lecture me for talking trash about Granny. He knew the score.

"I figured she wouldn't be able to make it," he said. "Still, we'll swing by at lunchtime and get you a change of clothes."

I thought about telling him not to bother. There wasn't anything in my drawers that could top what I was wearing. But then I thought about how it would make Granny squirm, and I warmed up to the idea.

I was starting to feel a bit partial to Mr. Hernandez. Before we went back to Granny's, we swung by Jukebox Joe's and he bought me a Manly Meal: double cheeseburger, fries, and a Coke so big it could float the *Titanic*. I allowed myself four bites of the burger, seventeen fries, and sixteen sips of the Coke before we crunched up Granny's driveway.

The crumb snatchers could smell the food on me as soon as we came into the hall, and before Granny could move her lard out of the chair by the TV, I slipped the bag—Coke and all—to Wolf Man, knowing he'd share it out fair and square.

Too late, I realized I should have counted the fries. At Granny's, food you could actually eat was as valuable as tailor-made joes in the joint. Wolf Man would have an easier time of it if I gave enough fries to divide equally between the crumb snatchers. I hoped he remembered Moonie Pie, too, who could easily jaw a fry.

"I told you she was nothing but trouble," we heard Granny say to Sink and Dip, flipping off the TV set on the kitchen counter. Granny and I had avoided each other since I tried to do her in with the ash can. Not that I was afraid. She had nothing on me in the felony department, and if she chose to drop a dime on Harry Sue, I could drop a dollar on her to the cops. The only thing that concerned me was what she might do to the crumb snatchers.

It is a well-known fact, Fish, that they are my weak spot.

Mr. Hernandez cleared his throat as she rolled into the front hall.

"The purpose of my visit, Mrs. Clotkin, is to inform you that the Marshfield EMS wants to honor your granddaughter, whose quick thinking may have saved the life of one of our students."

Granny looked suspiciously at Mr. Hernandez. She was holding the rubber ball she used to keep her hand grip strong and she squeezed it slowly.

Turning to Sink, she said, "What's he on about?"

I stood back, watching Mr. Hernandez take it all in. He was fingering his tie again, like he wanted to press it over his mouth. Granny's house was always too warm and the smell of poopy diapers mixing with the canned pea soup the crumb snatchers must have turned down for lunch would rival a humid day on the yard.

"He says that Harry Sue—" Sink began.

"I *know* what he said." Granny regarded Mr. Hernandez with a look that could corrode metal. "What does he want?"

I crossed my arms and waited. I hadn't had this much fun since the last health inspector found mouse poop in the peanut butter.

"Well." Mr. Hernandez cleared his throat. "Harry Sue's a bit of a hero around Trench Vista—"

He broke off and glanced at me, figuring in an instant I probably didn't share the highlights of my day over brownies and milk with Granny after school. So he gave her the long and short of it.

He finished with, "I'm told the papers will be covering it, which means—" Mr. Hernandez held out a piece of paper. "As her guardian, we'll need your permission."

"There any reward in this? Any money?"

"Well, I—I'm not sure. I don't think so. It's just a nice gesture. I wouldn't be surprised if there was a certificate. . . ."

Granny snatched the paper and pen and scribbled her name on the line.

"Better say where she lives," she growled. "Granny's Lap. Better mention we have openings."

She pushed the paper back at Mr. Hernandez, who, in return, gave her a look of pure astonishment.

Thinking back on it, it was the last time I had a good long look at Granny. That is, before my brains got scrambled and before the trial, where she did her best to appear old and feeble so the judge wouldn't send her up for long.

She glared at all of us, the skin under one eye twitching. She was giving us her lizard look: Sink, Dip, Mr. Hernandez, me. Like we were flies and her tongue was itching to connect.

It's not exactly a picture you want for your family photo album, but that's how I'll remember her.

"Well," Mr. Hernandez continued, "we swung by early to see if maybe Harry Sue had something a little more appropriate to wear to an awards ceremony."

Granny didn't even blink. She was a pro.

"Go find her something," she said to Sink and Dip.

"But . . . ," they responded in unison.

"I'm sure you got something she could borrow," Granny said calmly.

Now that I was going to have my picture in the paper and all, Granny realized it might not look so good for me to be dressed like I shopped at the Mercy Street Mission. So off went Sink and Dip, glancing over their shoulders at me, easily a good foot shorter and a bag of sand lighter than either one of them.

Chapter 29

We'll only stay a minute at the fire station. They had a little buffet, and ever since Baba, I was game to try new food. There was this nifty little appetizer: a slice of roast beef was spread with cream cheese and wrapped around an asparagus spear. I thought it would be slimy, but it was crunchy like a pickle and the meat was salty and fresh. There was a lady firefighter who noticed I was partial to them and wrapped some in foil for me to take home.

Violet was there with her parents, who hung around me like I was their long-lost daughter.

"Vi says you like chicken-fried steak," her mother whispered as the fire chief started talking about the history of the Good Citizen Award. I wanted to tell her I was partial to anything that wasn't burnt, spoiled, or otherwise too rank to eat, and also, could we please listen to what the man was saying about me?

I wanted to ask, did conettes get the newspaper?

Well, anyway, I could nab the copy out of the teachers' break room just in case.

I remember clear as a bell how I told myself it was okay to feel good about what I'd done. I *did* save a life. Just because I was the one who almost offed Violet in the first place was a matter to handle another time. You can't help it when people die. They just do. If you didn't mean to do it, then it's okay. Accidents happen.

At the moment, I thought it couldn't hurt to tell myself, *Good job, Harry Sue.*

And even though I wasn't around to see the picture they had in the paper the next day, I do carry it in the palm of my heart.

There I was, one arm around old Violet the Snitch, Dip's sweater hanging four inches down past the tips of my fingers. The Chumps were pressing in, big and soft, behind us. My other hand is shaking the hand of the fire chief. I'm looking directly at the camera and smiling, thinking how cheesed off old Granny's going to be when she sees what a fuss they made of me.

Chapter 30

I must admit I was feeling pretty high as Mr. Hernandez crunched up Granny's Loving and Licensed driveway. I had just begun to touch the idea of what it meant to *Live,* the way J-Cat said, with a capital *L.*

Maybe I wasn't doomed by all the bad that came before. Maybe it was possible to have a happy life even though both my parents had been sent up and my granny had an olive pit where her heart was supposed to be.

Life had delivered a KO punch to J-Cat, hadn't it? First, she got that bad sickness that kept her from having a baby. Then she fell for a guy who broke his neck in a ski accident and died three years later. But instead of giving up, she clawed her way out of the hole and spent most of her time pulling as hard as she could on Homer and Baba to bring them out with her.

In the end, she was a better road dog to Homer than I had ever been.

But hey, I was still a kid. I could improve.

Mr. Hernandez pulled away and I swaggered into the house. I had a sack of food in my hand and the crumb snatchers were going to get all of it. I'd let everybody have a bite of the roast beef asparagus thing and Wolf Man would share out the crackers and cheese while I told a story.

It was going to be a whopper this time, all about this lion who's supposed to be the king of the forest, only he isn't because he's forever trying to PC up.

Everybody was at the kitchen table coloring on some pages Granny had ripped out of the newspaper. Last year—even with Sink and Dip's entries— she'd failed to nab the winner in the *Marshfield Journal's* pumpkin-coloring contest, eight-and-under category. Granny wanted one of the crumb snatchers to win so she could lure in more unfortunate kids and their clueless parents.

I glanced around as Granny patrolled the kitchen table, whacking her ruler on the papers of kids whose coloring got a little sloppy. Even Hammer Head was bent to the task, his ears bright red, which suggested there'd been some fallout earlier.

Probably Granny was still furious that something good had happened to me.

I put my sack down. "Why isn't Moonie Pie down here?" I asked.

Sink was very busy coloring the stem of a jack-o'-lantern. I could have told her they weren't green off the vine, but I didn't bother.

"He was crying a minute ago," she said, without lifting her eyes. "But I think he fell back asleep."

I glanced around at the little kids, who didn't dare lift their heads even in greeting. They were coloring in slow motion, no pleasure in it at all. Carly Mae's little fist was in her mouth. Wolf Man could color a lot better than that.

A big lump grew in my throat. I tried to tell myself it was the cold medicine she gave before nap time, but I was pretty sure I'd scared Granny off that. No, the reason they were coloring so slow and so badly was because Granny had done something much worse. The crumb snatchers suffered from joint mentality. She'd taken the heart right out of them and they no longer believed things would be any different tomorrow than they were today.

It was what J-Cat said to Homer about sicknesses of the heart. They were worse than the pain Granny caused with her hands.

"I'll get him," I said, and walked out of the kitchen.

I stopped at the bottom of the stairs.

And that's when my whole life changed.

If somebody had cared enough to clip the picture of me from down at the fire station out of the newspaper, they could have written *Before* on it, because that day was the end of my life as I knew it.

Of course, not every kid's life ends two times before they hit their teens. But mine did. The first time was when Garnett Clotkin threw me out the seventh-floor window of Destiny Towers.

The second time was worse.

It took me a second—ten seconds—a minute—how do you know when time stops?—to figure out what was wrong with the picture in the hallway.

The stairs were shining.

And then I knew in a rush, following my eyes to the safety gate, listening to the noise of water dripping from one piece of wood to another.

He'd turned on the water. And something had plugged up the drain.

I took the steps two at a time, slipping in a puddle on the stairs, cracking my shin but feeling nothing.

Nothing but white-hot urgency.

The safety gate wouldn't open.

I kicked at it, but it held fast.

I jumped.

Never in my whole entire life will I forget the picture of Moonie Pie floating facedown in that bathtub. That picture grew me up quick. Up to that point, I didn't have much of a childhood and now I knew I never would. It was like the sun had sunk into the ocean and drowned, plunging the whole world into darkness.

From that point on, J-Cat had nothing on me. I went nut up.

I kept hearing the line in my head.

Don't hurt my baby.

And I knew I had to get Moonie Pie somewhere safe. I fished his fat little body—wet sleeper, swollen diaper, and all—out of the tub and took off, pressing him to me like a sponge.

I must have been screaming because I have this impression of them all at the bottom of the stairs, looking up at me with their mouths hanging open.

"Don't hurt my baby," I said, underlining every word.

Granny was taking the stairs two at a time. "Don't be a fool. He needs help."

I squished Moonie Pie to me harder and kicked at the safety gate. It caught Granny right in the shoulder.

Her howls joined mine as I bum-rushed her back down the stairs.

Somehow, she got a fist full of my hair. "Where do you think you're—"

"Hammer Head!"

I started screaming again. It was such a scream of pain and sadness, of the horrible agony I'd been feeling my whole life but had tried to hold in. It was coming out now and I couldn't stop it. Hammer Head launched himself at Granny and hit her right in the breadbasket. All the other little crumb snatchers swarmed her like killer bees.

"Get them off me," Granny was yelling, and Sink and Dip joined the fray while I shot out of the house like a cannon, leaving my road dogs to take care of Granny.

Don't hurt my baby.

I tossed Moonie Pie to my shoulder. One wet half dangled down my back as I held on to his slippered feet. Running. Running like my life depended on it. There was just one clear thought. I had to get Moonie Pie to safety. Hadn't Baba beaten back the lions? Hadn't he carried babies over swollen rivers and outrun soldiers with guns? If anybody could save us now, it would be Baba.

I felt something burst underneath my ribs and more warm wet liquid gush out, and I remember not so much thinking as *knowing* that my rotten old heart had finally burst with sadness.

I streaked across lawns and driveways and flower gardens and was to the edge of Baba's yard in less than ninety seconds from the time my toes left Granny's house of horrors.

There he was, standing just beyond the drive, hunched up against the cold in a brown leather jacket. I ran toward him, hurling myself forward, knowing me and Moonie Pie were just seconds away from safety.

As I crossed the driveway, I saw out of the corner of my eye a flash of shiny orange metal and I knew, with her recklessness and speed, J-Cat would not see us. Same as I knew that wanting couldn't make me move fast enough to get out of her way.

And so I passed him. I crushed Moonie Pie into a ball and passed him to Baba—using the now famous Clotkin chest pass—my love like rocket fuel, propelling him through the air.

And then the north winds and the south winds met where I stood. And I rose in the air. Me. Harry Sue Clotkin. At the eye of the storm.

Chapter *31*

Beau says, when an old con just up and dies, they handcuff his wrists together and put him in leg irons. They wheel him on a stretcher down the cell block, put him in an ambulance, and don't declare him dead until they get to the hospital.

They do it that way so they won't have to count him as dying in prison, see? It makes their records look better.

Most cons don't have funerals. The hacks just take a picture of the body with the handcuffs and leg irons still on. Then they bury him in the prison graveyard, unless somebody cares enough to collect him.

It could not have been that way with Garnett. I

just know it. There would have been too much blood. Young blood. He was only twenty-seven when he got shanked by a tat-sleeved shower hawk.

And it was my fault, too, because I should have told the judge that my dad had no impulse control. He was probably bumpin' his gums all over the place soon as they locked him in his cell. He didn't know how to collect road dogs. Probably what he did was nut up and eyeball a hack or drop a dime on the first con who got in his face. Poor Garnett.

And Mary Bell. She wouldn't have been so tired all the time if she didn't have a child to account for. Swing shift wouldn't have made her crank up if she ever got some decent sleep without a little crumb snatcher pestering her all the time to read and play games and all.

Those were the thoughts that haunted me when I couldn't sleep. They rattled after me in Granny's old house until I thought I was the one who would nut up.

After J-Cat hit me, dreams of Garnett and Mary Bell chased me all over, like two squirrels scampering up and down the walnut trees back of the house, only this time I couldn't escape them. I couldn't wake up. Morning wouldn't come.

And even after I began to hear, I still couldn't move. I still couldn't see. I didn't know they were keeping me that way for a reason, so my poor bones could pull back together one more time, so my swollen head would stay still.

I thought, *So this is my punishment.*

And it seemed right that I was struck down.

I couldn't keep track of anything: not time, not the people who were always coming or going, not even the pain that flared up like a match being held to different parts of my body.

I was in the special-handling unit. Shoe. The hole. No light. No words. Nothing but pain. Crazy maker. Nut up. Bug. Ding wing. Category J.

For once, I didn't fight it. I just gave up.

Chapter 32

First voice I could recognize was Mrs. Mead's.

"I'll be fine right here, Anna," she said. "The natural light is what makes it so nice to knit. I've done the death watch before, dear. My husband had four heart attacks before he finally succumbed. I can tell you from experience that a constant stream of communication is what pulls them back from the void. Harry Sue and I are going to have a little chat. About flowers."

. . . I'm partial to natives myself, dear, but there are some non-invasive exotics that I feel are truly worth sharing, particularly when you're gravely ill.

My, how she went on. Sometimes, J-Cat was in the room. I could feel her touching me. I couldn't stop it. She used some kind of cream, hot and thick, and rubbed it on my hands, pressing until she found the space between my bones and my muscles, pressing until I wanted to scream.

But afterward I paid attention to how good it felt, clean and free, like I was floating on a cloud.

. . . and I've discovered a whole new way of enjoying peonies. Paeonia suffruticosa. Tree peonies! They have stiff woody stems. No more lying on the ground to bloom. They'll stand up straight and tall. I've ordered three fuchsia sunsets for the garden. . . .

There was a new buzzing noise in the room, above my head, different from the machines that whirred around me.

And Baba's voice: "It will be too bright, Anna, you can't leave it on all night."

"I want her to see it in her dreams. I want her to know I'm communicating with her."

. . . Fortunately I was able to dig them up and overwinter them last year. But I'll never put them in the basement again. Good heavens, the earwigs! I thought it was an invasion. . . . No, all potted geraniums will remain in the garage from now on. . . .

And then I had the strangest dream. Aunt Em came to visit. Only she looked just like my grandmother on my mom's side, who died before Mom was sent up.

I wanted to ask her, "Aunt Em, would you still take Dorothy back if you knew the real story? About what she did to the witches and all? Would it matter that Dorothy didn't mean for it to happen?"

But it didn't seem right to upset her. And anyway, I couldn't make the words.

. . . It's always potatoes and peas on Good Friday. Any sooner than that and they'll rot in the ground. And if you didn't set your garlic in November, don't bother, dear. All you'll get is a lot of pretty top growth and a bulb the size of a lima bean. . . .

And then Homer was at my ear. "Lower, Baba," he said. "This is just between me and Harry Sue."

I felt his curls brush my cheek. *Who would push his hair back now?*

"You know I hate hospitals, Harry Sue, but I'm your dog, aren't I? Not just on the outs, but on the inside, too. Open your eyes, Harry Sue. That J-Cat's left a message for you."

. . . There is nothing more frustrating than blossom rot. I've spent more of my mad money than I care to count on those home remedies. In the end, I've given up on the tender things. What you need are the rot-resistant varieties, my dear. . . .

One morning, I felt the heat of her words on my face . . . and I smelled sunshine . . . and when I opened my eyes, I was blinded by a brilliant light.

And the thought came to me:

This is it. My eternal reward.

But then I began to focus. The hospital room came into view.

Over my bed hung letters, hot, flashing, orange neon letters. They spelled out:

LIVE

Part 5
Home

The Scarecrow listened carefully, and said, "I cannot understand why you should wish to leave this beautiful country and go back to the dry, gray place you call Kansas."

"That is because you have no brains," answered the girl. "No matter how dreary and gray our homes are, we people of flesh and blood would rather live there than in any other country, be it ever so beautiful. There is no place like home."

—*The Wizard of Oz*

Chapter 33

Most cons would say the time I did at Ottawa County General and after, at St. Mary Free Bed's Rehabilitation Hospital, was a catnap. Six months. That's not even serious change. But that was hard time, Fish, learning things any crumb snatcher should know. Like how to twirl spaghetti on your fork and how to pronounce words with *ch* or *ph* in them.

Living in that bed, it seemed like I was taking J-Cat's cure whether I wanted to or not. I was going back in time to before the fall. Like I woke up and I was five again, learning to put sentences together, learning to add numbers, learning to read all over again.

Life on the outs went on at a furious pace while

I lay in the hospital having the wires in my head un-crossed. Sink and Dip went home to mommy, Granny got stripped of her license and a catnap for neglect. She's doing all her time at the minimum-security facility down in Brownfield on account of her age.

Needless to say, I won't be visiting.

J-Cat lost her job as a home health aide for the county due to a history of disrespecting authority, and Baba's term as a substitute art teacher was up in the spring. So they decided to go into the child-care business together.

"I wanted to call it Deadwood Day Care, seeing as we got gimps and half-wits from front to back," she told me on her daily visit to make me practice flexion and build up the sorry excuse for muscles that were left in my body. "But Baba said it wasn't a good marketing concept."

And when he's not thinking up inventions, Homer Price comes down the ladder to serve good time with J-Cat and Baba in exchange for teaching the crumb snatchers all about the trajectory of a spitball.

Remember when I thought my poor old heart had broken for good on that sprint over to Baba's house? Well, I was wrong. That was the water gush-ing out of Moonie Pie's swollen lungs. I guess I didn't burn through all my luck during that fall. Ei-ther that, or knowing the circumstances of my crazy life, the celestial beings have given me more than my fair share. Soon as I'm ready, I'm due back at the Marshfield EMS to get me another certificate.

When the time came for me to get sprung from St. Mary's, I got a couple of sound offers for a place to flop. Ariel Dinkins said she'd take me in until Mary Bell had done her time, but so did J-Cat and Baba.

"I won't bring in as much as a day-care kid," I warned them.

"We got a mind you can work off the rest," J-Cat said. "Helping Baba in the kitchen."

"Telling stories to the children," Baba said, putting his arms around me. "They don't like Anna so much. She gets off track."

What with all the medical bills and the doctor visits, the social worker said it would be easier if they got legal guardianship over me until Mary Bell was back in the picture.

So as soon as they thought I could make the trip, we headed north to Gillikins, the joint that Homer and his girlfriends at the Wisconsin State Lottery had discovered was where Mary Bell was doing her time.

Chapter 34

As you might imagine, I had mixed feelings about seeing Mary Bell. Seems like everybody had an opinion about what she'd been up to. I guess I didn't know who to believe. The time had come for me to get my information from the source.

Every con and conette gets to make a list of the people who can visit. Fish, don't even bother adding those who cannot respect authority. I'm no expert in that department myself, but there is a look in the Harry Sue catalog for such instances. I've only called upon it once or twice since it seems to want to slide right off my face. It's a mixture of fear and stupidity with a little awe around the edges. It is a look that says, *Yes, indeed, O great and powerful Oz!*

I figured seeing Mary Bell was worth conjuring up the look.

I had never seen a prison for real, and I have to say that Gillikins and my imagination did not keep company on the subject. As we drove up, it looked like a big school or a hospital, with bushes and flowers and signs telling you where to park. But then, schools don't have fifteen-foot fences with razor ribbon hanging all over them, either.

And when we went inside, it reminded me more of an airport than a prison. Not that I've ever seen an airport for real, but I do have a television.

"Now don't forget to pee right before you go in," J-Cat said for the fourteenth time. "They're not gonna let you pee once you get in there. If you got to pee, it's over."

I don't really have any problems in that area, so I figured she was talking more to herself than to me. Baba had everything together in a file: my birth certificate, their foster-care papers and driver's licenses. Then there were the papers Mary Bell needed to sign *and* all the papers we had to fill out just to get in. Seems like it would've been easier to commit a crime.

Soon as we walked in the main entrance, Baba took my hand and we went up to a counter where a lady hack made sure everything was in order.

"Thank you," she said, stamping one of the

papers and handing the file back to Baba. "Have a nice visit."

She handed us a key on a chain with a big piece of wood on the end. "Everything in the lockers," she said, "except two dollars in change."

Baba already had the two dollars in his pants pocket. We could use that for the vending machines, he said. He found the locker with the same number as our piece of wood.

"Empty those pockets, Anna," he told J-Cat.

"I know the rules!"

After that, we found three plastic chairs against the wall and waited in silence. You didn't have to be there long to know the drill. The room was filled with waiting people: old people, crumb snatchers, T-Jones. Every so often the lady at the counter would say, "Visitor for Christina Switt will proceed to the security checkpoint."

Some group or other would pull themselves together and go to the metal detectors at the far end of the room. The rest of us shifted around a lot. I just couldn't get comfortable. J-Cat had bought me a new green blouse and shorts for the occasion, and they were making me itch something terrible. Every person I looked at, from the tired dusty visitors waiting to go through the metal detector to the man who was repairing the vending machine in the waiting area, might have seen Mary Bell since I had. Seemed like they were all looking at me funny. *Would she?*

"Visitors for Mary Bell Clotkin will proceed to the security checkpoint."

Baba took my hand and squeezed it. We stood up. The metal detector wasn't so hard. We put our change in a cup and went through. Then a man waved a wand over us just to make sure that machine hadn't missed anything. Big glass doors opened with a swoosh and we were in another room. Seemed like everything here was made of glass. I could see half a dozen hacks behind glass in a room filled with computers and other machines.

"Will you look at that," J-Cat said, pinching my arm. "It's like command central."

We had talked about this part in the car. Baba had talked, mostly to J-Cat.

"They have good reason to search us, Anna. *Your* job is to do as they ask."

"But I'm ticklish."

"Then don't come in."

"I'll behave," she said, crossing her arms and hunching down in her seat. I meant right then to tell her about the "Yes, indeed, O great and power-ful Oz" look, but she turned up the volume on the radio and we went on to something else.

I didn't like the lady hack touching me one bit, but it didn't matter so much when I told myself why. I'd had a fair amount of practice pretending I was somewhere else when the place I was seemed unbearable. So I let that guard look into my shoes and socks and then run her hands up and down my legs and my sides.

"Are you wearing a bra, young lady?"

"No," I mumbled, and looked down at the floor. Across the way, Baba looked just as miserable as me with some strange man's hands between his legs. But we got through it and stood aside, fingers crossed for luck, waiting for J-Cat.

She glared at the lady as she did her job.

"Are you wearing a bra, ma'am?" the lady hack asked.

J-Cat squinted. "You think I can carry this rack around without support?"

The lady hack put her hands on J-Cat's private parts. She reached into the neck of her sundress and pulled out a couple of tissues.

"What's this?"

"That's a snot catcher," J-Cat said. "Code name: Kleenex."

"What about *only* two dollars in change don't you understand?"

"You mean I can't bring in some Kleenex?"

"No, you can't bring in Kleenex. Those are the rules."

They each had a hand on the folded-up tissue that J-Cat had stuck in her bra.

"What if my nose runs while I'm visiting?"

"Use your sleeve. C'mon, you're holding up the line."

"Use my sleeve? Do you know where I got this turtleneck? Do you? Value Village, that's where! Cost me three dollars and ninety-nine cents!"

At this point, the guard took a step back and put her hand on the shiny brown stick hanging at her side.

Baba handed me the folder. "Allow me to apologize for my wife's behavior," he said, prying the tissues out of her hand and dropping them into the plastic tub on the table. He took her firmly by the hand and whispered something in her ear. J-Cat's wild eyes landed on me.

I was giving her my "please, please, don't burn the spot!" look. She shook her head to one side like she was trying to get water out of her ear. And smiled up at the guard.

"Sorry," she said, and sat down on the bench to put her shoes back on.

"I'd like to see her get snot out of a polyester blend," she muttered to herself.

"That's it, lady! You! Back here!"

With one shoe on, J-Cat jumped up and started stalking toward the hack, her fists clenched.

"Anna, please!" Baba said.

"You can take the kid," the lady hack told Baba. "But she's gotta wait outside. It's that or a termination. Make up your mind."

Baba and I held our breath. We both knew the

next ten seconds would tell us whether or not we had two conettes in our crew.

J-Cat's face was beet red, but she let another hack take her by the arm.

"Can I have my tissue back?" she asked through clenched teeth as they disappeared back through the swooshing glass doors.

The visiting room looked like the cafeteria at the hospital minus the food. There were more plastic chairs and round tables, and, at one end, another hack, sitting up high behind a wood desk so he could look down and see everything that was going on. Over in one corner, there were toys for crumb snatchers to play with and a fold-down table for changing the babies. Two little girls twirled an imaginary rope, while two more jumped between them, calling out, "Miss Mary Mack, all dressed in black," to use up their energy.

Baba and I stood on the edge, looking for somebody alone. Somebody with long dark hair who smelled like home. I thought I saw her, maybe. I touched Baba's arm. We started walking toward the lady who was chewing her fingernail and looking out at the crowd like she was looking real hard for somebody. As I got closer, it was all I could do not to throw myself into her arms.

But then we heard the words, "Harry Sue?" coming from another direction. I swung around, trying to find the voice, but I couldn't find a face that even came close to matching the picture I held in the palm of my heart.

Baba was walking somewhere. He turned back and put his arm around my shoulder.

"Is that my Harry Sue?" an old lady asked me. She sat at a chair against the wall, the fingers of one hand pressing against the other.

Black hair streaked with gray fell down around her soft face. She had on lipstick, but the lines weren't exactly right. It was the same with her body. There seemed to be too much of her for her head.

I looked at her, wondering how she knew my name.

Baba was close behind me, pressing me forward with his big hands.

I wasn't thinking too clear. My instincts took over. I started to run.

But I didn't get far because Baba had me again by the shoulders. He was pressing my face to his ribs, whispering in my ear.

"She's in there, Harry Sue," he kept saying. "She's in there."

And a little piece from *The Wizard of Oz* floated into mind. When some Munchkin asks Dorothy where Kansas is, she says: "I don't know, but it is my home, and I'm sure it's somewhere."

I forced myself to turn around and look *at* her. She was perfectly still, sitting on the chair. But I had never seen the look on that face before. She was crying, biting her lip and getting lipstick on her teeth. I can't even give you words for it, Fish, it was that far south of sadness.

Was this really my somewhere?

I stepped forward. "Mom?"

She made a little gulping sound and I ran into her then and crushed myself up against her and started crying like a baby, and we were just the same as the time I saw her before she was sent up. Only now it didn't seem so much like she was my mom, but like we were just two people, lost together.

When I finally pulled away, I sure wished they had let J-Cat come in with her tissues. Mary Bell had some, though, and she gave me one. Baba had moved away from us. He was being polite, giving us space. But as I watched him, playing peekaboo with a wandering crumb snatcher, I wished he was back by my side.

"I heard you been looking for me," Mary Bell said, trying to smile.

Fact was, Fish, I could hardly look *at* her. She had changed that much from what I remembered.

"You got . . ." I pointed to her mouth, and she laughed, twisting her tissue until it broke in pieces and rubbing it against her teeth.

"Guess you can tell I never wear it," she said. "I just . . . Well, I was trying to look presentable."

I wanted to ask why it mattered, after all this time. I didn't, but she seemed to know what I was thinking.

Mary Bell pressed her lips together. "I been such a disappointment, I know. I just thought . . ."

"There's something I gotta know, Mary Bell," I said, looking at my feet, forcing the words out of my mouth. "Did you . . . did you ever try to find me?"

Mary Bell wasn't in any condition to be talking. Her shoulders were working up and down like the seesaw on the playground and her face was twitching something terrible. I looked over at Baba, who'd lowered his hands from his eyes and was staring at her, too. It was so hard to watch that I left her face to study the little crumb snatchers calling out rhymes and pretending to jump rope in the corner.

If they could jump with no rope, I figured I could imagine my way out of this situation. I tried to use my mind to put a different face on the lady in front of me. But no other face would come.

"It's okay," I said finally. "You don't have to say."

"Baby," she said, sucking up her snot and rubbing the rest away on her sleeve. "I wanted you more than breathing, but I tried so hard not to . . .

not to be selfish. There were girls here said it wouldn't do you any good to see me, that you'd lose all your respect for me. That it was better for you to remember us like we were before."

I felt mad then, Fish, wondering what kind of waterhead goes to other conettes to get educated.

"It took me a while to find you after you moved. But I did. And when I called—you know we can't call except collect—Granny—" Mary Bell broke off there like just the name made her tongue burn. "Granny wouldn't accept."

Mary Bell covered her face with her hands and her shoulders started pumping all over again. When she finally looked up at me, her face was crumpled up just like that Kleenex she'd been worrying.

"Look what you went and did, Harry Sue. You went and grew up, anyway. And I had no part in that."

From out of nowhere, another conette slid into the seat next to Mary Bell and put her arm around her.

"That one yours, Mary Bell? I didn't know you had a kid."

Fish, there was so much churning inside me at that moment, I felt like a washing machine that's been dragged out of balance. Knowing Mary Bell didn't even talk about me to the other conettes was worse than knowing she didn't write those letters like I thought. It felt like . . . like, well, like taking a sucker punch to the heart.

I went over to Baba and pulled on his sleeve.

"I gotta pee," I said.

Chapter 35

I believe we drove thirty miles in silence on the way home. Baba held on to the steering wheel with his big hands and I stared out the window at the little streets that flew past as we drove along the one-lane highway. *What would I look like coming out of one of those houses?* I asked myself, desperate to keep from seeing Mary Bell's old face all messed up with despair. What about that one with the petunias in the wheelbarrow? Or maybe that one with the plastic windmill?

"Is somebody going to tell me what went on in there? Or don't you remember I was detained in the visitors' waiting room for over fifteen minutes?"

"Later, Anna," Baba whispered.

"Later? I been waiting for later since we left Gillikins. This *is* later."

"You can tell her," I said quietly, putting on a bike helmet in my mind and getting on that bike with the blue streamers.

I tried not to listen, but I found myself leaning forward more than once to catch Baba's soft words. When he got to the part about the conette who'd been ear hustling on me and Mary Bell and gave up that she didn't know Mary Bell had a kid, I pressed my head back against the seat. I didn't have to listen to *that* mess twice. I even closed my eyes.

That's why I didn't see what happened next. Baba says J-Cat stuck her little foot between his and slammed on the brakes. I smacked up against the door as he let loose swearwords from another continent and veered over to the side of the road.

She was screwed around in her seat as far as her seat belt would allow.

"Are you gonna let that flat-talking fool tell you how to feel about Mary Bell?"

I wasn't about to look at J-Cat. This was none of her business.

Do your own time! You nut-up-bug-ding-wing-crazy-making-Category-raggedy-old-J-cat!

I heard the glove compartment unlatch and the passenger door open. Then she was right beside me, banging on my window and waving a thick paperback book in my face.

"Roll it down! Roll it down!"

I looked at Baba. He was patting his shining face with a handkerchief.

"Let her have her say, Harry Sue, or we'll be here all afternoon."

I rolled the window down a crack with no definite plans to listen.

"You better listen!"

J-Cat kept her voice loud enough to override the hands I held against my ears as well as the cars passing on the highway. "This is your Kansas!"

She read:

The sun had baked the plowed land into a gray mass, with little cracks running through it. Even the grass was not green, for the sun had burned the tops of the long blades until they were the same gray color to be seen everywhere. Once the house had been painted, but the sun blistered the paint and the rains washed it away, and now the house was as dull and gray as everything else.

When Aunt Em came there to live she was a young, pretty wife. The sun and wind had changed her, too. They had taken the sparkle from her eyes and left them a sober gray; they had taken the red from her cheeks and lips, and they were gray also. She was thin and gaunt, and never smiled, now.

As she read, I started crying again and didn't care who saw or heard me. J-Cat yanked open the door and pushed in beside me. She pulled my head onto her lap and patted it.

"We don't know anything about it, Harry Sue," she said. "But I imagine your Mary Bell has been through worse than anything that old Kansas prairie had to dish up."

Being held by J-Cat is like getting a hug from a bundle of sticks. She is one bony lady. Soon as I recovered myself, I pulled away and tried to resume looking out the window on the other side. I needed to find somewhere else to be in my mind.

"There are a few things you don't know, Harry Sue," Baba said, making his way onto the highway again. "Things I learned after you left."

Since J-Cat was out in the lobby, they had let me leave the visiting room without Baba. He had to stay behind anyway to get Mary Bell to sign the papers.

"That woman was a new prisoner, a . . . how do you say it? A fish. She only just met your mother. And there is also someone who kept eyes on you while your mother's been in prison."

"What do you mean 'kept eyes'?" J-Cat asked. She had the window rolled down and was sticking her head out, feeling the air on her face.

"You know, watched Harry Sue. Kept eyes."

"Oh, you mean, 'kept an eye on her.'"

"I don't need a grammar lesson right now, Anna," he said.

"Just trying to be clear." J-Cat pushed her head out the window again.

But I still didn't get it.

"Stop the car!" J-Cat screamed, and this time she let Baba hit the brakes, believing after her wild call there must be some sort of emergency. Before we knew it, she was out of the car again, taking off down a side road just like the ones I'd been imagining myself on.

"What now?" Baba sighed.

I followed her with my eyes as she ran up the driveway of a small brick house with a sign out front that read: Free Puppies.

Not knowing what to do, Baba and I sat there, recovering, for quite some time, while a cloud of dust settled slowly around us.

"There were letters, too, Harry Sue. Not from Mary Bell, but to her. From Mrs. Mead."

I had no time to think this through since J-Cat came running back to the car and stuck her crazy orange head in the window.

"I wanna be Anna again."

"Huh?"

"Don't play me for a fool, Harry Sue. I know you call me J-Cat."

What was I supposed to say? It wasn't the most flattering nick in the world.

"Can I be Anna again?" she persisted. "I'm partial to it. That was my great-grandmother's name."

I nodded. Whatever.

She disappeared back up the driveway. Baba waited for me to ask about Mrs. Mead again. He wouldn't say more if I didn't ask.

"Mrs. Mead?"

"She wrote to your mother about you. And told her she'd keep you safe."

I wanted to know how old Mrs. Mead could keep me safe, but by now J-Cat was again back at the car, one of her kangaroo pockets squirming. Digging down, she pulled out the funniest-looking puppy dog I have ever seen, with black spots covering its stiff gray hair. Even though he was no bigger than a wood rat, his long tail poked up like the pieces of asparagus I watched coming up in Mrs. Mead's garden.

"Can he be Otto?" she asked, reaching through the window and plopping the dog in my lap. "I was going to be Otto, but then I turned up a girl. Otto was my great-grandfather's name."

Baba looked back at me and smiled. "Can he be Otto?"

"Okay," I said.

"That's a relief." Anna got into the car and

slammed the door. "Wasn't I saying this very morning, Baba, what we need is a dog?"

"What do you need a dog for?" I couldn't help it. I bit.

"Why, to lick up Homer's tears. That's what for."

Chapter 36

There's only one piece of literature worth taking to the hole and that is *The Wizard of Oz*. If Louise Frank Baum were still alive, I'd write him a letter. That is some kind of story.

I hope someday you read that book and get educated, Fish. Because every time I do, I learn something new. I've had brains and lost them, tried to lose my heart but kept it, and hated those monkeys with a passion until I learned the backstory. They were under a spell.

All the while I was lying there in that hospital bed, my mind kept coming back to Dorothy. I know what the Tin Man was missing, and the Scarecrow and the Lion. I'd always figured what Dorothy was missing was Aunt Em, but it isn't true. In the end, I figured out that Dorothy's problem was not about getting sprung from Oz.

You have to work harder to figure out Dorothy's mess. But there is a clue. It comes right after she meets Scarecrow and Tin Man. Dorothy listens to the two of them bumpin' their gums about whether it's better to have brains or a heart. After listening for a while, she thinks: "If she could only get back to Kansas and Aunt Em it did not matter so much whether the Woodman had no brains or the Scarecrow no heart, or each got what he wanted."

I tell you, Fish, that just slayed me. What kind of a road dog did that make Dorothy? No kind, that's what.

But by the end of the book, you wouldn't catch Dorothy caring so little about her friends getting their deepest wish. Not after they saved her gingham-checked butt from witches, Quadlings, Kalidahs, wolves, bees, Winkies with spears, and what all.

We don't know what Dorothy got up to after she landed back in Kansas. But you can be sure she wasn't the same Dorothy who left in the eye of that storm. And whatever new road dogs she met up with, well, at least she'd know how to treat 'em.

Chapter 37

There's a yellow line all around the edge of the exercise yard in the joint, and cons call it the "yellow brick road." That's right. Unlike Dorothy and her crew, cons and conettes don't so much want to walk the yellow brick road as get beyond it to their new life on the outs. It helps some to know, finally, that my Mary Bell is not as far away as Oz is from Kansas. She's just beyond that yellow brick road.

It's late summer as I write this, and I'm still recovering, mostly here in Mrs. Mead's garden. Me and Moonie Pie got a little catching up to do in the brains department, so I bring the crumb snatchers down every day and we weed, and pick runner beans, and cut flowers to put into mason jars.

Homer's inventing a birdbath that cleans itself, so Baba props him up in a lawn chair on the edge of the garden to contemplate it. Once we got back from Gillikins, Anna kept Homer and Otto together night and day, so that pup won't go much farther than the pillow they tuck under Homer's right arm.

"You ever get the urge to be Christopher again?" I asked Homer, feeding him *koftah,* the little meatballs Baba had taught me to make that morning.

Otto was sitting up at attention, waiting for his share.

"Why would I want to do that?"

"I just thought since J-Cat wanted to go back to being Anna . . ."

"But *she* didn't change, Harry Sue. She's Anna because *we* changed."

"I don't follow."

"She's always been Anna. We gave her that nick because we were doing time, not her."

Otto's little face was turning this way and that, from my hand to Homer's mouth and back again. I pinched off a bit of meatball with my other hand and let him take it from my fingers.

"I can never be Christopher," he said sadly. "There is no more Christopher."

"But you're the same person on the inside," I insisted. "You didn't change on the inside."

"Yes, I did, dog. I sure did."

And his eyes started to leak a little, and Otto

278

was on that like a duck on a June bug, as Mrs. Mead says, like he was born to the task of washing Homer's face and making him giggle like a crumb snatcher.

Homer's words got me thinking. I always was Harry Sue, wasn't I? On the inside and on the outs.

"Homer," I said, "I got a favor to ask you."

"Okay."

And so I told him what had happened that very morning while I was cooking breakfast with Baba.

"Your mother gave me something for you during our visit, Harry Sue," Baba told me. "But she asked me to wait until you had time . . ."

He broke off talking to pinch the *kisra* in the pan with his fingers and flip it over.

"Time for what?"

I could see he was searching for the right word.

"To reflect."

It was a slim little book. A spiral-bound notepad. There was my kindergarten picture on the cover, and around it were designs, doodly hearts, and curlicues. Lots of them. And there was my name in fancy letters. Harry Sue.

"It is a book of poetry she wrote for you," he said. "But also to remember you. Now she wants you to have it."

I left Homer on the lawn then and went to get the little book. I got his breakfast tray, too, the one that let him turn the pages with his chin.

"You always did have my back, Homer. Now somebody's gotta read this book before me. Because I don't think my heart is strong enough to handle any more surprises."

Homer nodded. "Better take Otto," he said. But that was all he said. Because in a very deep way, Homer knew just what I was feeling.

I *have* changed, Fish, but I will never be Harriet Susan. Because in the eyes of the first person who really mattered, I was Harry Sue.

And I just had to make sure I still am.

But we didn't have time to talk about those deep things because, just after dinner, Mrs. Mead came to collect all of us: Baba, Anna, Homer, Otto, Mrs. Dinkins, and me.

"It's the time I was telling you about all the winter long, Harry Sue," Mrs. Mead said. "Do you remember it? *Ipomoea alba?*"

She seemed so excited that I nodded yes, but I hadn't the faintest idea what she was on about. We sat on Mrs. Mead's back porch, making small talk while it got dark. Baba held Homer gently in his big arms. Anna kept jumping off the steps, trying to catch fireflies, and Otto ran around her feet, snapping at the little flashing lights.

"Anna," Mrs. Mead said finally. "Settle. Now close your eyes, everyone, and sniff."

We did.

"At night, the flowers have to rely on scent to attract their pollinators."

Anna sniffed again. Loudly. "It's divine," she said.

I smelled it, too, like someone had sprayed perfume in the air.

"Now look there." Mrs. Mead pointed to a small clump by the step. With all the tramping I'd done up and down her stairs that summer, I don't know how I could have missed the beautiful white flowers whose blossoms were reflecting the moonlight.

"These are the moonflowers I was telling you about, Harry Sue." She plucked a flower and handed it to me.

"All winter long I was telling you that some things require the dark night to bloom."

I took the flower over to Homer and pressed the silky petals to his cheek before holding it out for him to see.

"Look, there's a star in it," he said, and we both saw rays of a different shade of white peeling out from the center of the flower, forming the shape of a star.

Lighting up the night from below, just like a miracle.

Notes and Acknowledgments

Straighten up, Fish.
It's time to act like your T-Jones taught you
something and thank the people.

Let's begin with my first, most brilliant and sensitive critics, my sons, Max and Walter Gilles, who at this writing are fourteen and twelve. I couldn't ask for better readers. My husband, Roger Gilles, and my dear friends Terri McElwee, Debra Nails, and William Levitan all gave invaluable input. I can't thank you enough for your close reading and your honesty.

My expert panel includes Pam Lockwood, piano teacher extraordinaire and former home health nurse (whose methods bear no resemblance to J-Cat's), and Joe Abramajtys, a fellow writer and former prison administrator who helped me see what I could not. I would also like to thank all the children of prisoners I have met along the way. Thank you for sharing your fantasies, your hopes, and your fears with me.

In addition to Joe and my young friends, I learned Conglish from a number of excellent sources. Books like *Doing Time: 25 Years of Prison Writing*, edited by Bell Gale Chevigny, and *Undoing*

Time: American Prisoners in Their Own Words, edited by Jeff Evans, were great sources. So were the excellent *True Notebooks* by Mark Salzman and *Behind Bars: Surviving Prison* by Jeffrey Ian Ross and Stephen C. Richards. The glossary in *Behind Bars* gave me the idea for Harry Sue's "Joint Jive" glossary. All of these books are written for adults. If you want to share a great book about prison with kids, check out *Life in Prison* by Stanley "Tookie" Williams. This is where I learned about "J-Cats" and many other details of daily prison life.

You should know, dear reader, that while Harry Sue is a composite of many girls, all the major events in this novel are based on true stories. My files are filled with news clippings. The summer I began *Harry Sue*, a young girl was thrown from a seventh-floor window by her father—and lived. A baby drowned in a bathtub where she'd been laid for a nap by her child-care provider. A foster grandmother was arrested and later convicted for severely abusing the children in her charge. And a woman in Florida was convicted of accidentally giving a baby in her care a lethal dose of Benadryl, a cold medicine, to make her sleep longer. Horrible things do happen every day, and I want to acknowledge the grief of those who've lost children due to abuse or neglect.

Even though there is cruelty, neglect, and sadness in our world, there is even more compassion and altruism. To young people, I say thank you for being kind to each other. The human heart is very fragile, even when it appears to be covered in riveted steel. Also, my deepest gratitude goes to the adults who care for children, who teach them and who work with juvenile offenders. Your kindness and your sympathy for the hard task of growing up make a world of difference.

I will never forget the magical day almost twenty years ago, when I witnessed the wedding of our old family friend, Rick Stein, to his wife, Leah. Paralyzed in an accident as a teenager, Rick as the leading partner in their wedding dance on wheels was a moment of pure joy for all who witnessed it, proving that the human capacity for love can overcome even the greatest obstacles. And, no, for the record, Leah did not nail her grandmother with the bouquet. I just can't mention real people in relation to J-Cat without making clear that she is a fictional character without a human counterpart. Unless we count me.

In Dorothy's story there are two good witches, but here in Grand Rapids we have many! I would like to particularly thank Debbie McFalone, the executive director of Curriculum and Elementary Instruction for the Grand Rapids Public Schools (GRPS), and Julie Powell, fine-arts coordinator of GRPS; Dorothy Johnson and Shelli Otten, principals in GRPS; Sarah McCarville, youth-services coordinator for the Grand Rapids Public Library; Sally Bulthuis and Camille DeBoer, owners of Pooh's Corner Children's Bookstore in Grand Rapids; Terri McElwee, of Elite Karate and Fitness; Gretchen Vinnedge, education coordinator for the Community Media Center; Molly Corriveau, a celebrated artist and professor at Kendall College of Art and Design; Mary Jo Kuhlman, Ball Foundation; Jane Royer, corporate volunteer coordinator of the United Way; and Susan Heartwell, executive director of the Student Advancement Foundation. Trish English and Mary Johnson are outstanding volunteers, mothers, and friends.

Okay, okay, we'll have some honorary good witches, too: Bert Bleke, superintendent of schools for GRPS; Fritz Crabb, community programs manager at the United Way; Steve Robbins of S. L. Robbins and Associates; and Sherman McElwee of the McElwee Martial Art Center. You are my crew, and every day you work hard to make a difference for kids in our city. Thank you!

Thank you always to Mom and Dad and Marge for all your support, and to Suzie and Johnny for my beautiful Waterman pen, which has written two novels now.

To my road dog—and dog-loving agent—Wendy: my back has never felt the breeze since we started doing good time in 1993. And, finally, to Nancy Hinkel, my dear friend and editor: meeting and working with you and your colleagues at Knopf is like putting on the green spectacles in the Emerald City. Your wit, sensitivity, and charm—not to mention your keen fashion sense—make everything perfect.

Oh, and my deepest apologies to L. Frank Baum, whose first name is really Lyman. I have always loved *The Wonderful Wizard of Oz,* both the book and the movie. It is our most creative and enduring American fairy tale. I love that it is a classic quest story with a girl as the protagonist. During the creation of this book, both Nancy and I felt strongly that we should weave a bridge between Harry Sue's story and Dorothy's adventures in Oz. What other word can be made from the letters in Otto's name, for instance? Why does Mrs. Mead kiss Harry Sue? Who begins the book with the ability to fix everything, but ends up just an ordinary human? We have left countless details for you to discover. There's even one in the map of Oz. Happy hunting!

But most importantly, in connecting with the characters from Baum's story, Harry Sue is doing what librarians and passionate readers have always understood: stories can sustain us in times of great trouble. They comfort and inspire. I hope we never lose sight of the importance of imagination and of stories as a tool for combating despair.

When *The Wonderful Wizard of Oz* was published

in 1900, the *New York Times* wrote: "The time when anything was good enough for children has long since passed, and the volumes devoted to our youth are based upon the fact that they are the future citizens; that they are the country's hope, and thus worthy of the best, not the worst, that art can give."

My sentiments exactly. Somehow I think Harry Sue's intense involvement with his story would both flatter and amuse Lyman. *The Wonderful Wizard of Oz* is truly worth reading again and again.

About the Author

Sue Stauffacher's first novel for Knopf, *Donuthead*, received starred reviews from *Publishers Weekly*, *School Library Journal*, and *Kirkus Reviews*, which declared it "touching, funny and gloriously human."

In addition to writing children's books, Sue is a speaker on the issues of literacy, bullying, and creating a more compassionate culture, drawing on her work as a journalist and educator for more than fifteen years. Visit her Web site at www.suestauffacher.com for the *Wizard of Oz* "cheats," the map of Oz, and other fun stuff that makes reading come alive. Hint: Toto's got the Easter eggs. Sue does good time in Grand Rapids, Michigan, with her husband, Roger Gilles; her two sons, Max and Walter; her dog, Sophie; and her cat, Fig.